Neutral Zone

by
USA *Today* bestselling author

Catherine Gayle

.

Dedication

This one is for all of my readers who've been begging me for a book for Colesy since I released In the Zone. I always said I wouldn't write it until and unless the right story idea came to me. I'm glad it finally came to me.

Chapter One

Luke

"Cheer up, buttercup," Dani said, pulling out a chair at our parents' dining room table and sitting across from me with a smirk. She was my younger sister—almost twenty-one to my almost twenty-four—and she had always had a knack for getting on my last fucking nerve.

Today was proving to be no different.

It was just like during all those long summer vacations in the back of our parents' car, driving across the country to see whatever national park or monument they'd decided we needed to see.

And, just like in those days, I was sorely tempted to yank on Dani's hair or pinch her arm until she cried. But she was apparently pregnant, and I doubted her husband, Cody Williams, would appreciate me doing anything of the sort.

Too bad pregnancy hadn't made my little sister any more tolerable, although a guy could hope that maybe motherhood would do the trick. Lord knew nothing else had.

Instead of making her cry, I glowered at my food. "Why the hell should I cheer up? I still don't have a contract." I stabbed at the sliced berries on my plate, but one of the fuckers slipped away from my fork and shot across the table like a projectile. Would've served Dani right if it'd hit her, but I had no such luck.

Not in any area of my life, apparently.

The berry landed on the table in front of her. She picked it up and popped it in her mouth. "Yeah, but Dad said there'll be all sorts of pro scouts hanging around during training camp. Someone'll notice you. They have to. Everyone knows who you are, so they just need to see what you can do."

Fat chance of that happening. "They already had plenty of opportunities to see what I can do. They saw. They didn't care. They moved on." But I still hadn't managed to move on yet. Hell, I might never manage it, because playing hockey was the only thing I'd ever envisioned myself doing with my life.

I'd played four years of college hockey at the University of Minnesota, and no pro team in North America had taken a chance on signing me to a contract after graduation—not even any of the minor-minor-league teams, the ones that paid a hundred bucks a week and shipped their teams around on broken-down busses, the ones where fans got into beer-tossing fights in the stands because that sort of thing was more entertaining than the action on the ice.

Then I'd gone off to play for a season in Germany.

It'd gone well enough, I'd thought. But not a single damned NHL scout had done so much as talk to the coaches about me. They'd been around my games. They'd noticed some of my teammates. But none of them had given a shit about me.

I'd tried to catch the attention of some of the bigger European leagues, like the Swedish Elite League and the KHL in Russia. No dice. They didn't care.

If none of them were interested, then there was little wonder why no NHL team wanted anything to do with me.

And I knew exactly why all of these teams weren't interested, too. It had nothing to do with me not being good enough and everything to do with me not being straight enough. I'd officially come out of the closet in my senior year of college, and all of a sudden, scouts had stopped coming to watch me play.

Poof. Gone, just like magic. No one had any interest in the gay kid.

Sure, everyone said my sexual orientation had nothing to do with it, but it was the only explanation that made sense to me. Maybe I wasn't as skilled as my father had been, but I had the same fucking work ethic and I wasn't a damned liability on the ice. I knew how to be a good teammate, and no one tried harder than me. No one wanted it more than me. Playing pro hockey was the only thing I'd ever dreamed of, for as long as I could remember.

There were plenty of guys playing in the NHL who weren't as skilled as I was and even more who didn't put in the kind of effort I did on a daily basis. So why had they been given a shot, but not me?

I reached across the table and grabbed another of Mom's biscuits, loading it up with butter and some jalapeño jelly, choosing to stuff that in my face rather than speak to Dani. Then I scooped another healthy pile of scrambled eggs onto my plate, stacked a few sausages next to the eggs, grabbed a banana, and refilled my coffee cup before heading outside with my breakfast. I'd much prefer to gorge myself in peace and quiet rather than having to listen to Dani try to cheer me up.

The screen door swung shut behind me. I set all my food down on the table beneath the umbrella and pulled one of the chairs closer, sitting with my back to my parents' house.

No sooner did I have myself situated than the screen door opened and slammed shut again.

"Seriously, Dani, I'm not in the—"

"Can't say I blame you," her husband said, which surprised me just enough that I turned around to see with my own eyes that it was Cody Williams and not my sister. We all called him Harry because he looked so damned much like the British prince—well, everyone except Dani called him that, at least. Harry took a seat next to me and gave me a commiserating look, passing a beer into my hands and opening another for himself.

"Isn't it a bit early in the day for a beer?"

"Not if you have to deal with Dani."

I snort-laughed. "Truth."

"Pregnancy hormones are making her more obnoxious than normal. Or at least I'm choosing to blame it on the hormones."

"I don't know how you live with her."

"Some days, I don't either. But other days…" He shrugged. "We're good together. Good for each other."

"Well, I'm just glad she's in your hair and not mine."

"She's got a point, though," Harry said.

I glowered at him over my coffee mug, then eyed the beer and opted for that, instead. "I'm not willing to concede anything when it comes to Dani."

"Yeah. Siblings." He grinned and leaned back in his chair, teetering on the back legs the way all the guys and I used to do in elementary school. "Good thing we don't have to live with them anymore as adults, even though we can't quite live without them, either."

"Your sisters are a hell of a lot easier to deal with than mine." I'd met them briefly last year, when I'd been home from Germany for his and Dani's wedding. His sisters were normal. Dani…well, Dani was about as bullheaded and obstinate as they come.

"Every family has a unique dynamic," he said.

I snorted. "Yeah. *Unique.* That's what we'll call her."

"Seriously, though. Come skate with us. Quite a few of the boys are back in town already. We're all getting ready for the new season. Lots of scouts will be around. You never know what'll happen."

"Yeah. Sure."

But he was wrong. I knew exactly what would happen.

Nothing.

Not a damned thing would come from me skating with those guys.

Maybe it'd help me get into game shape, but what good would that do me if I wouldn't be getting into any games?

So even though I'd agreed to go, I wasn't sure I would.

He raised a brow. "You don't sound like you're going to follow through with it. Do I need to get a few of the boys over here to drag you up to the ice?"

In lieu of answering, I downed about half my beer.

"Mm hmm," he said, scowling. But then he took another swig of his beer and leaned forward. "And you're coming with us tonight, too."

"Tonight?"

"For karaoke. We're all going to Voicebox."

Karaoke? Oh, hell no. That seemed like my worst nightmare come to life. Or maybe my second-worst nightmare, since I was already living the absolute worst. "Sounds like something Dani dreamed up," I muttered.

"Yep. And she's making me go, so I'm making you go. Well, technically, I'm inviting you. But if you don't get off your ass and come along of your own free will, I'll get Jonny to take care of it for us. You're coming."

Jonny was better known as Cam Johnson—the Storm's resident enforcer. The guy could easily bench-press me if he wanted to—and I wasn't exactly small.

Lovely.

"I guess I'm coming to karaoke tonight, then."

"I guess you are."

"Just don't expect me to get on stage and sing," I said.

"I think your sister's going to make us all do it."

"Dani?" Seemed like something my younger sister would do. She'd always been a bit of a brat. Actually, that was putting it mildly.

"No, Katie."

Katie was the singer in the family.

And Harry sounded miserable about the thought, unless I was sorely mistaken.

"Dani's teaming up with her, though," he said. "Combined, they're a force to be reckoned with."

"Don't I know it," I grumbled. "I've had to live with the pair of them a hell of a lot longer than you have."

"Yeah. So in other words, you know you're getting up there and singing, whether you like it or not."

Fuck. Looked like I was going to karaoke night.

Cole

"I kissed a boy, and I liked it," Koz sang into the mic, drunk off his ass while the rest of us looked on in some combination of amusement, disgust, and horror. I was caught between amusement and horror, but disgust was starting to creep into the equation. He kept making all sorts of crude gestures as he sang, grabbing his balls and flicking his tongue toward anyone who dared to look.

Several of the guys' wives and girlfriends rolled their eyes and went back to a table far away from the karaoke stage, where a few of the other Portland Storm WAGs had already gathered.

"Ignore him," Keith Burns said next to me, his voice just loud enough to carry over the din of the karaoke club. He took another swig of his beer and tugged his wife, Brie, closer to his side.

"Always do," I replied. Ignoring Koz was something of a full-time job for me. Hell, for a lot of the guys on the team, actually. If he weren't such an effective pest on the ice, we might not be so willing to put up with his antics off it. But there was something to be said for the way he could get under the skin of just about anyone on the opposing team at any time he wanted.

"He's just being a fucking ass," Burnzie said.

"When is he not an ass?" I demanded.

He shrugged. "Good point."

"The only point that matters," Brie put in.

Burnzie and Brie had come back to Portland early for the new hockey season because Brie was due to pop with their next baby at any moment, and they didn't want to be in the middle of packing and moving when that happened.

I was back early because I was working out with the team's trainers and taking more dance classes at Brie's studio, all in the name of improving my core stability so I could be more effective on the ice. It'd been working out well so far, but I knew I still had a good deal of room for growth.

A lot of the other guys with families had already returned because their kids were starting school and whatnot.

None of us could figure out why Koz was here already, though.

He should be in Cancun or Greece or somewhere else, having a good time and being a jackass, as usual— but doing it far away from the rest of us. Somewhere we didn't have to put up with it yet.

Somewhere he'd be out of my reach.

He was too damned close right now. It wouldn't take very many steps for me to grab him off the stage and strangle him—a thought that made me a bit too happy.

Being a jackass was about the only thing he was good at other than playing hockey. Lucky for him he could make a living from hockey.

"When is Babs going to do something about that guy?" I asked, trying to sound casual even though all of us knew it was anything but a passing question. Babs, otherwise known as Jamie Babcock—the Storm's captain—was the only guy on the team who could keep Koz in line. For the rest of us, it was all we could do to keep from ripping the guy's head off about fifteen times a day—or double that amount on a bad day.

"Do you honestly think anyone can rein him in?" Burnzie asked. Then he flagged down a waiter and signaled for another round.

Brie gave me a commiserating look. "They just got back from Babcock Central, oohing and aahing over Cadence's sonogram. He's probably not in the mood to do anything about Koz right now."

Cadence was married to Levi "501" Babcock, younger brother to the aforementioned team captain, and another of our teammates.

The waiter dropped off our drinks.

I reached for my wallet, but Burnzie shook his head. "It's on me. Anyone who has to suffer through that fool's shenanigans deserves a free beer," he said, indicating Koz up on stage. He shoved a credit card into the waiter's hand.

"Or three," Brie added. She put a hand on the small of her back and shifted, a look of complete discomfort on her face.

Normally I liked to pay my way, but tonight I was just frustrated and pissed off enough to let Burnzie buy me a couple of rounds. "So Cadence is pregnant, huh?" I asked, trying to carry on the conversation and forget about Koz. Not easy, since the douchebag was still flailing all over the stage to a mixture of hilarity and shock from the audience.

"Yeah, but I don't think I'd say too much in front of Babs and Katie," Burnzie said.

Our captain and his wife had been trying—unsuccessfully—to have a baby for a while now. At least for a few years. Anyone paying attention could see how it was wearing on them and straining their relationship.

I nodded my understanding and thought about drinking my beer.

"Maybe we shouldn't talk about that right now," Brie said quietly, but her gaze had shifted to somewhere behind me.

I casually looked in the same direction and found Luke Weber—Katie's younger brother and the son of one of our coaches—heading our way.

But Luke wasn't merely part of the extended Storm family. He was also a hockey player.

And he was gay.

Like me.

Luke had officially come out of the closet not long before I did. His revelation had taken the hockey world by storm, blazing the trail for me to follow. To be honest, I wasn't sure I'd have had the balls to do it until after I'd retired if he hadn't come out first.

I sure as hell never intended to. It was supposed to be my little secret—well, mine and a few select friends and family—until having my sexual orientation out in the open wasn't likely to have an effect on my career any longer.

Life has a way of screwing up even the best-laid plans, though. I didn't regret coming out. Not *really*. My teammates had been great about it, and while there were a few jackasses around the league, for the most part it wasn't an issue. No one cared.

But Luke had opened that door, and then I'd followed him through it, and there was no going back.

Not for either of us.

Luke plopped down in the empty seat next to me, looking miserable. Adorably miserable. Not that I had any business thinking of him as adorable, but his pout made me think things I had no business thinking.

I shoved my beer in his direction since I hadn't started drinking it yet. The guy looked like he could use it more than I could. And it gave me something to do other than think about kissing the pout off his face. Now was not the time. Hell, there would never be a right time for that. And this definitely wasn't the place. But a beer? Yeah, I could give him a beer.

He raised a brow.

"Rough day?" I asked.

He scowled. "How much longer do you think I have to stay so my sisters will get off my case?"

"Depends why they're on your case," Brie said.

"Doesn't matter. They're my sisters. It's their favorite pastime—giving me a hard time."

"Haven't seen you up on stage yet," Burnzie pointed out. "I think they'll throw a fit if you try to weasel your way out of it."

"I don't care. I'm not making a fool of myself just to appease them," Luke shot back. "The talent gene skipped over me."

Bullshit, I thought to myself. Luke had plenty of talent. The guy was a damned good hockey player. He was just undersized, and this was a tough business to make it in. Very few smaller hockey players got a shot because there was always someone bigger and faster.

"Might make your life easier," I pointed out. I wished I had sisters like his, who'd be on my case about things. A family who cared. The guy had it all—he just didn't realize it.

"Just be glad you're not related to them," Luke said.

I couldn't help but let out a small laugh, despite the sharp, sudden-onset pang of longing I felt. I'd give my left nut to have sisters and parents like his. But I managed to pull myself together before I said anything about it. This wasn't about me; it was about him. "You don't have to go along with them, either," I said.

"I do if I want to have peace."

Burnzie snorted. "Peace is overrated."

Koz was finishing up his song, which meant Katie and Dani were bound to be on the hunt for someone to force onto the stage next. I quickly scanned the dark room, trying to spot them. Sure enough, they had their heads together and were looking our way—but a sea of bodies would prevent them from getting to us too quickly.

"Wanna make a run for it before they grab you?" I asked.

His face lit up for a moment, but then he came crashing back down again. "I've had too much to drink. I can't drive."

"Good thing I'm sober," I said. "Let's get out of here."

"Yeah?" He glanced back over to where his sisters had their heads together, and then quickly downed the rest of the beer. "Let's go."

Chapter Two

Luke

As if it wasn't bad enough that I was as jealous as all get-out of the man driving me home, halfway back to my parents' house, my years-long crush on him was starting to get the better of me, all due to staring at his hands.

In other words, I had the boner to end all boners, and I was trying to casually hide it beneath the jacket I'd awkwardly draped across my lap.

And I was almost positive I was failing.

To Colesy's credit, even though he was bound to have noticed my problem, he kept his eyes on the road. His radio was tuned to my favorite station, and he kept tapping his fingers on the wheel in time with the drum beat—hence my current obsession with his hands.

"Did you ever play?" I asked.

"Play?" He cocked his head toward me in question as he pulled to a stop at a red light.

"Drums." I nodded, indicating the way he was pounding out the beat on the wheel, but that only made me pay attention to those hands more than I already had been. They were long and strong, with a few calluses here and there. A man's hands. A hockey player's hands. A working man's hands. Not overly manicured or pretty or perfect.

Studying those hands made me hotter than I already was. I shifted my jacket again, trying to keep things hidden.

His lips quirked up in a grin. "Believe it or not, in middle school, I was in band. Played percussion. I was always better at playing the keyed instruments than drums, though—xylophones, marimbas, that sort of thing. And I really enjoyed playing timpani."

I didn't even know what timpani meant, but I chose not to reveal my ignorance. "So you never played on a set? Never had a garage band?"

Colesy snorted in laughter. Damn, that was hot.

"Nah," he said. "My dad would've been thrilled if I'd started up a rock band as a teenager, though, even if it meant noise and drugs and partying. Maybe if I had, I wouldn't have been such a disappointment to him."

"How the hell could you be a disappointment to anyone?" I demanded. "Least of all, your parents." As far as I saw it, the guy had everything.

Or at least everything I wanted.

He raised a brow and studied me, and a waft of his cologne hit me out of the blue. Damn. He even *smelled* good—like a clean breeze with just a hint of spice. And I was clearly too drunk to be trusted around him.

"Not everyone has a family like yours," he said.

"You should be glad about that."

He half laughed, turning back to stare out at the streetlights. "I'd give anything to have a family like yours, Luke. You have no idea how good you have it."

I wondered what he meant by that, but Lady Gaga's "Bad Romance" came on the radio, and he reached over and turned up the volume, effectively cutting me off before I could get started. Then the light changed to green, and when he started driving again, we both sat there with nothing but Gaga's tune keeping the silence at bay.

The song faded out and the DJ was just coming back to the mic when Colesy turned the corner onto my parents' street. It killed me that the drive had been so short. I wasn't ready to go inside. Wasn't ready to get out of his car. I wanted to stare at his hands and breathe in his cologne and bask in the glow I felt from having his attention all to myself for a lot longer.

"You're lucky, you know," he said.

"How do you figure that?"

He slowed down and then came to a stop next to the curb in front of my parents' house. Then he faced me, one arm draped casually over the steering wheel. "Because your biggest issue is that your sisters want you to sing karaoke, to loosen up and have some fun."

"My biggest issue is that no one'll let me play hockey."

"No one's stopping you from playing hockey. Maybe they're not going to pay you for it, but they're not stopping you from playing."

"You know what I mean, though," I groused.

"Sure, it sucks. But it's not the worst thing that could happen. And you know it. Look at all the shit

Katie went through. Look at what Harry and Dani are dealing with for his dad. You know things could be worse."

"Now you're being all mature and level-headed on me." And I got the sense that he was avoiding saying something that was eating at him, but I didn't have the first clue what it might be. Cole Paxton had always been one of the quieter guys around, and he kept his private life private. That was possibly the biggest reason that coming out the way he had was such a surprise to everyone. It was completely out of character.

I knew he'd done it to take the heat off a friend and teammate, too, which only made me respect him for it all the more. The guy had a hell of a lot of character. He'd done something that put him under a microscope, which was the last thing he wanted, but he'd done it anyway.

He gave me a half laugh, which only made him seem hotter to me. "You coming to skate with us tomorrow? Harry said you were."

"I don't know, man. Not really feeling like it."

"Then maybe all those scouts who passed on you were right. Maybe you don't have what it takes."

Ouch. I reached for the door handle, but he stopped me by putting a hand on my elbow, which shot tingles of awareness down my spine. I didn't turn to face him, because there'd be no chance I could hide what he was doing to me.

Fuck, I was a mess. Even when he said something to sting my pride, I wanted him. I wanted to be like him. I wanted to be *with* him.

"I don't really believe that," he said. "You know I don't. I don't think anyone does—but I've never taken you to be a quitter. Never thought you'd give up so easily."

"Maybe you don't believe it. But I'm starting to think I do." And with that, I climbed out of his car and headed inside before he could say something else that would make me feel like an ass.

Cole

When I walked into the Storm's practice facility the next morning to get in some ice time and a session in the weight room, I took a quick glance around to see if Luke had decided to show up.

Then I immediately wished I hadn't looked, because Koz had set up a yoga mat on the floor—not far from our logo in the middle—and was doing yoga.

Naked.

More specifically, he was in a plow pose, his ass high in the air and his limp dick dangling between his legs.

"What the fuck are you doing?" Hammer demanded, nearly stumbling into me from behind. Hammer was what everyone called Chris Hammond, my regular defensive partner and the oldest veteran on the team. "No one wants to see that shit."

He had a point. Maybe none of us were overly concerned about jumping in the showers together or changing clothes, but that didn't mean we wanted to see more than was necessary.

"Naked yoga," Koz shot back. "What does it look like I'm doing?"

"You look like you're trying to suck your own dick. Probably the only way you can get a blow job."

"You're just jealous, old man," Koz responded, without breaking form. "You wish you looked this good naked. Come to think of it, maybe you should learn to do it. You probably can't get a good blow job these days. Need to learn to service yourself."

"If anyone in this room can't get any action," Brenden Campbell said as he lumbered into the room and slipped past me, heading for his stall, "it's you. Because you don't know when to shut the fuck up."

"Fuck you, Soupy," Koz shot back at him.

"No thanks. I'm good." Brenden Campbell, better known as Soupy, tossed his gym bag in his stall and started stripping down to get ready to skate. "Come to think of it, though…you seen any action lately? Maybe that's why you're behaving like more of a fucktard than usual. Got blue balls."

Koz lifted his hand to flip off Soupy, somehow avoiding falling down, while all the guys laughed.

Damn, it was good to be back around these boys. Maybe they got on my last fucking nerve sometimes, but these days, they were my family.

I skirted around Koz to get to my stall, determined to ignore him, even though the jackass made it next to impossible to do anything of the sort. Nicky Ericsson, our top goaltender, was already suiting up two stalls down from mine.

"Kids all ready for the new school year?" I asked, pulling my pads into place.

"Nils is starting middle school and Hugo's a freshman now. Elin's got a new boyfriend every time I turn around, and I don't like any of them. And if that's not bad enough, Molly thinks she's a teenager, too."

"Molly's just a toddler," I said, trying not to crack up.

"Two going on twenty. She thinks she's as old as Elin and can do all the things Elin gets to do. She's got a boyfriend. Some three-year-old kid at the park. I'm not ready for this shit."

I laughed.

"Just wait till you have kids," he said.

Fat chance of that happening, but I chose to let it slide. The guys were good about treating me like I was just like the rest of them, which was nice, even though I wasn't.

The door opened again, and I glanced over my shoulder. Harry's bright-red hair was the first thing I saw, but just behind him, I caught a glimpse of Luke Weber looking somewhat less sullen than he had last night when I'd dropped him off at his parents' house. He met my eye for a brief moment, with a flash of some indeterminable emotion shining in his eyes, before he turned and followed his brother-in-law to an empty stall so he could change.

Good. I might have pissed him off last night, but not enough that he was going to completely avoid me.

I finished changing and headed out to the ice to stretch, having a hard time keeping the grin off my face.

Chapter Three

Cole

Since training camp hadn't officially started yet, the coaching staff couldn't be part of any workouts or on-ice sessions we took part in. That was why Luke and a handful of other unsigned hockey players were allowed to join us.

The coaches were still watching us, though, and we all knew it. They would surely be looking down from their office windows, and any number of scouts from around the league and Europe would drop in to see how everyone was skating and who looked like they might be a useful acquisition to fill a hole on their own roster.

Which was precisely what Luke was counting on. He needed to catch someone's attention and show them that he had exactly what they needed, that he could fill wherever needed.

We were a hodgepodge group of returning Storm players, veteran NHLers who lived in the area and were still hoping for a contract for the upcoming season, and younger guys like Luke who just hoped to catch on somewhere and make it stick.

In the early part of the week, we just tried to get our skating legs back after not getting on the ice much over the long summer months. Luke and the handful of younger guys skating with us had a leg up on guys like me, Hammer, and Soupy.

We were all on the wrong side of thirty-five, and it took a lot more effort for us to get back in the swing of things—and to recover after a workout. More and more often, I resorted to soaking my entire body in vats of ice water, in hot tubs, in Epsom salt baths, just to keep things moving like they should be.

Even though Burnzie and Jonny were up there in age along with us, somehow the two of them didn't seem to be suffering from the same effects. I had to admit to some jealousy as far as that was concerned, but at least I didn't seem to be as bad off as Soupy. The guy was lucky he could get out of bed most days, but still, he kept coming in and putting his body through the same hell, day after day, year after year.

Our group had decided to have a full scrimmage on Friday afternoon since training camp was due to start on Monday. This would likely be the last time this particular group of guys would all be together to play, so we wanted to go out with a bit of fun.

Since Nicky was the only goaltender we had among the group, we decided he'd be a skater, just like the rest of us, and we would put up a shooting target in each goal. The four corners and the five-hole were our only options for scoring goals.

"If I'm skating, you all have to play out of your normal positions, too," he argued. "Defensemen have to play forward, forwards have to play defense."

"Fine," Koz said, "but you're playing forward."

"Why not put me on *D*?"

"We're going to have too many defensemen and not enough forwards. So you're up. We might still have to leave a couple of forwards playing forward." Koz looked around, counting heads.

Don't ask me why we were allowing him to be in charge. Still, for some reason, everyone agreed. This was going to be insanely ugly hockey, but probably a hell of a lot of fun—a lot like a game of pickup hockey on the pond when we were kids.

By Nicky's rules, Luke ought to be playing defense, but with Koz's rule change and the fact that he was one of the extra guys practicing with us who wasn't actually a part of our team, he got thrown out there as a center. He was naturally a right wing. I wasn't sure if he'd ever been slotted in as a center before.

"Be good for you," I said, skating out beside him for the opening face-off. "More practice taking draws, and lots of scouts are watching."

He didn't respond other than to look out into the small set of bleachers surrounding our practice ice, which were relatively full of scouts from around the league. Hammer lined up opposite him. I set the puck down between them and took my position, and they rhythmically tapped their sticks against one another's stick and then the ice three times before taking the draw.

Luke won it cleanly, but that wasn't saying much, since Hammer probably hadn't taken a face-off since he was a teenager, if then. Luke sent the puck back to Soupy and we headed into the zone. Koz tried to trip me up, so I took a good whack at his ankles with my stick.

He bounced back up with his trademark grin that always meant he was about to stir up some shit. "No slashing, douchenozzle."

"No tripping, fucktard," I shot back.

He just grinned and took off.

Despite myself, I grinned, too. Damn, it was good to be back on the ice. Even if it meant I had to deal with Koz.

Luke

I always hated to admit that Dani was right, but this time, she was. Not that I'd ever tell *her* anything of the sort. The whole city of Portland wouldn't be able to contain her ego if I did. Hell, her head probably wouldn't fit inside the entire state any longer.

But whether I wanted to concede a point to my brat of a sister or not, I definitely needed to get back on the ice again.

Hockey was a part of me. I felt alive in my skates and pads and gloves. My hands curled around my stick and felt like they belonged there—far more than they ever would have grasping a microphone and stepping in front of a camera, like Katie, or coiling around a pair of scissors and working at a sewing machine, like Dani.

This was where I was meant to be, what I was destined to do.

It had to be.

Besides, the cool air on my cheeks served to wake me up in the mornings a hell of a lot better than any amount of coffee could, and there was nothing like a hard crash into the boards to get me revved up for the day.

On the ice, skating with the Storm players and the other unsigned stragglers like me, I found that I could breathe again—deep, full breaths, for the first time since my agent had told me he couldn't find any takers and to sit tight while he worked the phones. And that had been more than a month ago, with no news since. Playing hockey was the only thing that felt right, whether I had a contract for the coming season or not.

The future was still hanging over my head, though. Or rather the giant question marks about *my* future. Did I have one to look forward to? Would I find a team willing to take a gamble on me, or was I bound to be washed up already before even reaching the ripe old age of twenty-five? And if, God forbid, I couldn't make a career for myself through playing hockey, then what?

Yeah, I had a bachelor's degree in journalism. I honestly had no earthly idea what I intended to do with it, though. I'd only majored in journalism because I'd had to be working toward a degree in order to play college hockey, and it had seemed like a decent backup plan.

But I'd never intended to *need* my backup plan. Who did?

I'd thought college hockey would be my best bet at garnering the notice of pro scouts, and I'd get into the NHL, and then after a decade or two of playing pro, I'd move on to whatever came next. The goal was to use that journalism degree *then*, maybe moving into hockey commentating or something.

I didn't want to need it now.

Maybe it was a good thing I'd gotten a degree, after all. Looked like I might need to make use of it sooner than planned.

After the goal-heavy scrimmage—which ended at twenty-four to seventeen, and Colesy and I had been on the losing side of it—everyone showered and headed out to have lunch at Amani's. It was a local family-style Italian place where a lot of the Storm players liked to eat before games.

I went with them because I didn't want to deal with Dani, and chances were high she'd be stopping in at Mom and Dad's house today. She seemed to come by every day lately, and I wasn't entirely sure it was just due to my return from Europe or if there was something else afoot. She had a really bad habit of trying to set people up on dates, and from what I could gather, her setups didn't often work out all that well. I had no intention of becoming her next victim.

When I arrived at Amani's, there were two open seats remaining—one next to Colesy down at the far end and the other near the middle of the table next to Koz, who was looking at me with an expression I didn't want to interpret.

I booked it over to claim the empty seat beside Colesy.

He winked at me when I sat down, which did a number on me. Good thing he couldn't see what I had going on beneath the table. Spending so much time around him lately wasn't helping my crush. Far from it.

"You know," he said, passing a basket of garlic bread over to me, "your agent could maybe try to sell the idea that you could play as a utility player somewhere—defense when needed, but you could also fill in as a lower-line forward sometimes. Maybe there's a team out there who needs someone like that."

"I've never played defense before in my life. And just because I took a few face-offs in a shinny game…" I let the thought trail off, shaking my head.

He shrugged. "It'd be worth a shot. Hammer and I can give you a few pointers for playing defense."

Hammer leaned across the table and grabbed the salad tongs, putting a large pile of greens in his bowl. "First pointer: get really good at skating backwards without falling on your ass or needing to look behind you. Second pointer: get really good at falling on your ass."

"Third pointer," Nicky said, "talk to your goaltender."

"Nah," Hammer said. "No one wants to talk to him. But it's a good idea to talk to your partner."

Nicky rolled his eyes. "And you wonder why you don't get more ice time."

"I get plenty of ice time," Hammer said. "They put me in an ice bath after every game."

"Because you're an old man," Soupy shouted from the other end of the table.

"Never said I wasn't. But seriously, you've got to talk on the ice."

"Honestly, though, there's a lot more to it than that," I said. "And I've never been good at taking face-offs. I'm shit at them."

"You did all right today," Hammer said.

"Yeah, against *you*."

"Point taken." He stuffed his face with a garlic roll and gave me a shit-eating grin.

"We could have you and Koz work on those face-offs," Colesy said.

"I don't want to do anything with Koz."

Even though he was all the way at the other end of the long table, it seemed the jackass in question had heard me saying his name. He looked up and gave me a crazy look before stuffing a meatball in his mouth.

I did my best to ignore him. "For real, though. If working on face-offs with him is my best shot at getting a contract…"

Colesy chuckled. "He's an ass, sure. But he's a damn good center. You could learn a lot from him."

I scowled.

"Think about it, okay? What'll it hurt?"

Only my pride.

"Who's talking about my ass?" Koz shouted. "Colesy? I knew you liked me. You probably can't help it. I'm hot."

"A hot fucking mess, more like," one of the other guys muttered.

Colesy flipped Koz off.

And that was when it hit me like a box of pucks being dropped on my head—*this*. This kind of thing was what I'd miss most if I couldn't keep playing hockey. Sitting around, shooting the shit with a bunch of guys, taking jabs at each other…

My gut twisted into knots, stealing my breath.

"Yeah," I said. "Yeah, all right. I'll try to learn to play defense."

"And practice face-offs," Colesy said.

"And I'll practice face-offs." And I'd even practice them with Koz, like Colesy had suggested, because I didn't have any better options.

Chapter Four

Cole

"You've got to cheat as much as possible without them calling you for cheating," Koz said, leaning low over the ice, his legs wider than his shoulders to give him stability. "And keep your body as close to the ice as you can. Think about how Crosby does it."

"Crosby gets away with all sorts of shit that no one else does," Luke muttered.

"Because he's that fucking good," I said, watching the pair of them from behind, in the same position I'd take for a face-off in a game situation. "If you get to be as good as he is, you'll get away with just as much. But until then, you've got to do everything to the letter. You're not getting low enough."

"Just think about it like sex," Koz said. "If you're

gonna take it in the ass, your ass has to be available."

"You're about to take my fist in your face," Luke ground out.

Koz laughed. "Good. Better than your dick anywhere near my ass. Seriously, though. Get pissed off at the guy across from you, but use it to win the face-off. Channel it to get the job done." Then he nodded at Soupy, who was acting as the linesman.

Soupy dropped the puck, and Koz won it cleanly. Luke had barely reacted, and the puck was already halfway down the ice.

"You were watching the puck," Koz said. "Big mistake. You've got to watch the linesman's hands."

"How am I supposed to see the puck on the ice if I'm watching his hands?"

"You're not. If you wait until you see the rubber hit the ice, you're already too late."

Which was one more reason why *I* would have never made it as a center. I could react to a trio of forwards skating into my defensive zone and put myself into the right position to help out my goaltender, but trying to win a face-off when the puck was still in the air? Good thing I wasn't the one trying to learn.

Soupy dropped the puck again, and Koz tied up Luke's stick, circled around, kicked the puck out of the face-off circle, and knocked Luke on his ass, all within the span of about half a second.

"How the fuck am I supposed to learn anything if you're always kicking my feet out from under me?"

"How the fuck are you supposed to improve if you're not competing against someone who's better than you?" Koz shot back. "I don't practice taking face-offs against Nicky—I practice against RJ, because he's better than me. Besides, that's something a lot of guys will do—come in to knock you off your skates and take you out of the equation. You've got to learn how to deal with it."

Luke got up, glared at Koz, and put his stick on the ice again. The two of them took draw after draw. Koz kept up a steady stream of advice mixed with insults and chirps in a pattern no one could predict without living inside Koz's head. The guy was definitely an ass, but he could rein himself in relatively well, as long as he had somewhere to direct his attention. Right now, his attention was fully on helping Luke learn to take face-offs. Surprisingly, he was a good teacher—not something I ever thought I'd say.

About halfway through our time on the ice, some movement in one of the windows up above us caught my eye. I looked up and noticed Luke's father, Storm assistant coach David Weber, watching us with an inscrutable expression. Proud papa? Or was he thinking this was all pointless, that I was getting Luke's hopes up for nothing? Hell, maybe he wasn't even watching us to see what was going on with Luke, at all. He might just be observing to see how the guys on our team were looking, since the preseason would be starting soon. We didn't have much longer to prepare for the upcoming season.

The good news was that Webs wasn't the only one watching. About half a dozen scouts had shown up this morning, from teams all around the league. This was what everyone had promised Luke would happen. It was what he needed.

Quite a few of our other teammates had started coming back to town, since training camp would officially start in a few days. At that point, Luke would be on his own—he couldn't keep skating with us anymore. He'd have to find somewhere else to skate and someone else to practice with, so he needed to put his best foot forward now. He'd have no better chance at making an impression.

After a solid hour, Luke was clearly tired, dripping with sweat, but at least he was gradually showing signs of improvement. No one got to be good at taking face-offs in a single day, though, so he had a lot more work ahead of him.

"Enough for today," Koz said, tapping Luke on the shin pads. "Be sure you stretch. Your quads are going to be sore like a bitch after that." Then he skated away to take a few laps around the ice.

When Luke turned to me, it was with a look of utter defeat. "This is never going to work."

"It might. Lots of scouts watching you up there."

He scowled like he didn't believe me.

"Gotta have faith," I said. "Come on. Koz was right—you need to stretch or you'll be hurting later."

With a sigh of resignation, Luke finally headed for the tunnel. I followed him, but on my way, I happened to glance up and see his father watching me with a familiar expression.

It was the same way he'd always looked at Babs whenever Katie was around, back when she was a teenager and young adult. He'd given Babs those looks for years before they'd gotten married. It was the same way he'd looked at Harry any time Dani was flirting with the guy. The way he had always looked at those two just before telling them not to be an asswipe, trying to scare them away from his daughters.

My stomach twisted in knots, and not because I was scared of David Weber.

I didn't want to get involved. Not with anyone. Not until I retired.

It was bad enough being the only openly gay player in the NHL—something I'd never intended to be. I didn't like carrying this mantle. I didn't want to blaze a trail for others to follow. I just wanted to quietly live my life, and once I'd retired, then I could do whatever felt right. *Then* I could get into a relationship. *Then* I could do whatever the hell I wanted, and I wouldn't have to worry about the media circus that would follow.

Wasn't it bad enough that the whole world already knew I was gay? I had no intention of inviting them into my private life any further than they'd already come.

But with the way Webs was looking at me…

It was like he saw something that I didn't want him to see. Like he saw something I didn't want to admit to myself.

Like maybe there was something more than just me wanting to help Luke.

Why should I be so invested in him? He was just another hockey player with big dreams who had never quite made the cut. He was no different than any of the other guys who'd come to skate with us over the last couple of weeks.

Was he?

There wasn't any good reason for me to be taking him under my wing if there wasn't more to it than that. Even I could see the truth when it hit me like a Chara slap shot straight to the noggin.

Well, hell.

Luke

I'd never spent this much time around Cole Paxton before, and it was seriously doing a number on me.

Yeah, a bunch of other hockey players from in and around the Portland area were with us, too, but still. It seemed as if, regardless of who else was with us, he and I had been constantly together over the last few weeks.

We worked out together. We had lunch together. We hit the weight room together. He was always trying to find ways to help me improve my game, too.

Hell, one morning, he even came into the locker room carrying two cups of coffee—one for himself, and he handed the other to me. "Skinny mocha with an extra shot of espresso," he said.

"How'd you know my coffee order?"

He shrugged and headed for his stall to change clothes, leaving my stomach doing jumping jacks.

"Thanks," I said meekly.

And then I wondered what his coffee order was so someday I could return the favor. I made a mental note to ask Jamie. He'd probably know. My brother-in-law tended to notice a lot of the little details about people. It was why he made a good captain for the team. And maybe if he didn't know, Cody would. It was worth a shot.

A couple of days later, Colesy walked in with a pair of shot blockers that he handed to me. "I accidentally ordered more than I needed," he said. "Thought maybe you could use them."

I decided not to point out that I wouldn't have any need of any hockey equipment at all if I couldn't sign a contract somewhere. Mentioning that seemed churlish and ungrateful, and I didn't want to be anything of the sort when it came to Colesy.

Instead of being able to handle my infatuation better because I was getting to know him as a person, the opposite was happening—I was in over my head and drowning in my crush.

I kept catching myself staring at him across the ice and forgetting what I was there for and trying to finagle ways to spend more time with him. Even the sound of his voice was enough to send me reeling for a while.

Mainly because he was such a good guy.

Some people, once you got to know them, you realized they were assholes underneath it all—like Koz. To be honest, I'd never understood how my brother-in-law put up with the guy, but Jamie had always gotten along well with people no one else could.

With other people, they were too wrapped up in themselves and the shit going on in their own lives, so they didn't have time to spend on getting to know anyone else. Or maybe they were so focused on their careers that they couldn't see past the ends of their noses. (I tried not to think about myself falling into that category, but I feared there might be some truth to it.)

With Colesy, though, the more I got to see who he was on the inside, the harder I fell.

I was a fucking mess—focusing more on getting to know him than I was on proving myself to all the scouts hanging around. I wanted to bask in his presence and soak him in. I wanted to learn to be more like him.

I wanted to be with him.

But that wasn't something I could have. Not if I also wanted to continue pursuing a career in hockey.

I knew better than to think the Storm's coaching staff and the general manager would suddenly discover they had a spot on their roster that I could fill just because of who my father was. I didn't want that, anyway.

I wanted to blaze my own trail in this business and not get by just because of my family connections. I wanted to earn my spot. I hated the thought that anyone might think I'd only been signed because of my father being one of the coaches.

And even if I forgot all about my career (or lack thereof), there was still the not-so-small matter of not knowing whether Colesy would want the same things I did. He'd always led a relatively private life for someone in the spotlight. Maybe he was already in a relationship and just kept it to himself. Maybe he didn't want to get into a relationship until he'd retired because he didn't want to deal with the media circus that would surround him if he did.

Maybe he didn't have any interest in me in that way.

In all fairness, that last part was likely true, whether the others were or not. The guy was about a decade older than me. Maybe he was just being a nice guy because that was who he was—a nice guy—and it didn't have anything to do with an attraction to me.

But no matter what was behind his actions, I couldn't deny that he seemed to be going out of his way to help me. Every time I turned around, he was offering another suggestion for how I could catch a scout's notice, trying to help me learn a new position or hone a new skill, texting me the contact info for some agent or scout or exercise specialist who might be able to give me a leg up on other players in the same situation.

The more he tried to help me, the less I wanted his help—because if, somehow, I managed to sign with a team, it would mean I'd have to leave.

I didn't want to leave. I didn't want to be halfway across the country from him, or worse, on some other continent entirely.

I wanted to be with him.

The two things I wanted most in the world right now might as well both be impossible, and even if I managed to get one of them, I knew I couldn't have both.

If I got a contract, I'd have to leave.

And if I found the cojones to do something about my crush on Colesy, I'd have to give up on playing pro hockey. It was a lose-lose proposition. No matter which prospect I pursued, I'd have to give up one for the other...and I might end up missing out on everything that mattered to me.

The last day before training camp officially started arrived. All of the Storm's regulars had come back to town, the other stragglers had gone off to wherever they were headed for the new season, and my agent still hadn't called me with any offers.

Not that I was surprised, exactly. Disappointed would be more accurate. Or heartbroken.

I got up, the same as normal, and headed down to my parents' kitchen for breakfast. Dad had his iPad on a stand in front of his plate of bacon and eggs with a side of fruit. Video footage was streaming on the screen.

I tried not to look because I knew it was bound to be something that would make my chest ache, but I couldn't seem to stop myself as I headed for the Keurig to fix a cup for myself.

Then I really wished I hadn't looked, because he was watching film from the scrimmage we'd had a few days ago.

"You need to get lower over your knees on face-offs," he said, not bothering to look up. "You could get more leverage that way."

"Doesn't matter now."

"It might. Teams are still looking to fill holes."

I grabbed a container of yogurt out of the fridge while my coffee brewed, then pulled an apple out of Mom's fruit basket on the counter.

"Come here," he said, backing up the film.

"I don't want to."

He acted as though he hadn't heard me. "You need to see this for yourself. Then you'll understand."

"I already understand. Koz and the rest of those guys drilled it into my head. It's not that I don't get it—it's that I'm not good enough."

"You don't even know what I'm going to show you. Just get over here."

My coffee had finished brewing, so I didn't have a good excuse to stay away any longer. Damn it. I carried my meal over and took a seat next to my father. "What?" I said, hating my sullen tone but incapable of stopping it. "You want to show me how I'm watching the puck? I know I'm supposed to watch their hands."

"Just shut the fuck up and look, okay?"

Glowering, I took a bite of my apple and stared at the screen.

He pressed Play, and the video started up again. I saw myself from the side, easily standing half a body length taller than Koz across from me, and consistently swiping for the puck about a quarter-of-a-second later than he did, which made me too late.

"Know what I see there?" Dad asked after a few minutes of this. He paused the video and pushed the iPad away.

"Me sucking."

"Actually, no. I see you trying. But that's not what I was talking about, to be honest."

"Then what? You want to tell me I'm too slow? Too small? I already know all of that. They've been telling me for years. Hasn't changed anything."

He hit the rewind button and backed it up. When he hit Play again, he zoomed in—but not on me. "What I noticed is Colesy."

My throat went dry and swelled closed so I could barely breathe as I started to watch it again, my attention fully on my crush. And *his* attention was squarely on me. Every move I made, his eyes followed me. He shifted his body almost in time with mine, as if he could anticipate my every movement before I'd made it.

I felt as if my heart would pound through my chest, so I took a big gulp of my coffee to see if it could calm my nerves. "So what?" I said when I thought I could trust my voice. "He's a good teacher. He was just trying to help me out." Wasn't he?

"Whatever you say, kiddo," Dad said, pushing his chair back from the table.

"That's all it is."

"Maybe. But maybe not."

He carried his dishes to the sink and then gathered his iPad and the gym bag he always took with him to practice. Before he went out to the garage, he stopped again, leaning against the counter and staring at me.

"What?" I asked, unable to finish eating my breakfast because of the whirlwind going on inside my stomach.

"What do you want, Luke?"

I shook my head, trying to shrug off his question because the truth hurt too much to give it voice.

"Answer me," Dad said. "What do you want—*really* want?"

"I don't even know, anymore."

"I don't believe that. Not for a second."

Of course he didn't—because he was my father, and he knew me too well to believe a lie that bold.

"The things I want are things I can't have," I finally replied. I got up and took care of my dishes, too, because it gave me something to do—a way to avoid the heat of my father's intense scrutiny.

"Your mother and I always wanted you to believe you could have anything you wanted if you worked hard enough for it," Dad said, sounding gruff, as if he might get choked up if he wasn't careful about how he worded things. "We wanted that for all of our kids. We wanted to make it true. But sometimes, life isn't very fair. Sometimes, good people don't get the things they deserve. Sometimes, hard work isn't enough."

"I know that." I turned on the faucet because I was afraid I might start crying, and I didn't want to cry in front of my dad. Or I might start yelling at him, and he didn't deserve that.

"I wish I could make the world a bit more fair for you."

"It wouldn't *be* fair if you got involved. I have to figure this out on my own this time."

"I know you do. It's killing me, though. I always wished I could wave a magic wand and make the world a better place for the three of you, but it doesn't work that way. Your mom and I've had to take a step back and let you all go out into the world and make your own mistakes."

I froze. "I didn't make a mistake. Coming out wasn't a mistake. Being gay isn't a mistake."

"That's not what I mean."

"Then what?"

"I'm talking about letting you pursue a career playing hockey."

"You did it," I bit off. "Worked out all right for you."

"I was lucky. It was luck more than skill or ability."

"Luck, skill, ability, hard work, dedication, determination..." I stopped there, but I could have kept going.

"But a lot of luck," he said. "The cards lined up right for me. It could have easily gone the other way."

"But it didn't."

"No. It didn't."

I finished loading all the breakfast dishes into the dishwasher and dried my hands on a towel before turning to face him. "What would you have done if things had gone a different way?"

"Good question. I didn't have a backup plan. I didn't go to college like you did. Jumped straight into the AHL and worked my way up from there. And if the coaching gig hadn't fallen into my lap after I retired, I honestly don't know what I would've done with myself. I'd be floundering, probably still to this day. And I'd be driving your mother batshit crazy while I was at it. She got used to having me out of her hair because of hockey so she could pursue her own interests. We work well together this way." He stared at me so hard it left me squirming. "I don't like to see you floundering. You need to figure out your backup plan. Find out what makes you happy. Figure out what'll help you feel whole."

Without hockey, I didn't think anything would ever make me feel whole.

Chapter Five

Cole

As soon as the rest of the team returned to Portland and training camp got officially underway, Anne Golston and her *Eye of the Storm* crew were back in action, too.

They'd been following us around with their cameras for long enough now—about a season and a half—that I should have been used to the feeling of invasiveness. But in my life, things rarely worked out the way they should.

It creeped me out every time I felt a lens zooming in on me or saw a cameraman shift into a different position so he'd have me from a better angle.

It felt as though I were living my life under a microscope.

The way I'd come out of the closet in front of those

very cameras had only heightened my sense of unease. It was probably just a figment of my imagination, but these days, it always seemed as though they were filming me to an inordinate degree more than they filmed most of my teammates.

I didn't want to be a story—or at least not because of my private life. I wanted the team to be the story, or maybe one of my teammates.

Anyone but me.

So I put my head down and focused on the task ahead of me—preparing myself both mentally and physically for the upcoming season.

The mood around our locker room was upbeat this year. We'd come really close to winning the Cup last year. There hadn't been too many changes to our roster over the off-season. Our core, the heart of our team, was still intact. Hockey pundits everywhere were saying this was our year, but more than that, *we* believed it.

Every person in the organization, from our general manager to the coaching staff to the players and even down to the training staff and equipment guys, believed we would be closing out our season by skating the Stanley Cup around the ice. And then we'd follow it up with a huge, celebratory parade through the streets of Portland.

All of that was at the forefront of my thoughts, but I couldn't get Luke Weber and his plight to play hockey somewhere this season off my mind. It was easy to put myself in his shoes and imagine what he must be feeling. It could easily have been me in that same position. I'd never been the biggest or the best. I'd never been a shoo-in for crafting a sustainable career in the NHL. Hell, in all the years I'd been in the league, I'd rarely been more than a serviceable third-pairing defenseman who could occasionally play in a bigger role to cover for injuries.

So why had I made it and Luke couldn't? In the end, it all boiled down to luck, or maybe to being in the right place at the right time. Some coach or scout along the way molded me into a player who could fill the need they had, and I'd been filling that same role ever since. And Luke... I supposed he just hadn't had that magic moment yet, when all the stars aligned just right. He hadn't shown the exact skill that the right team was looking for or something.

His father had played in the league for about two decades and had gone straight from playing to coaching, so Luke had been around the hockey community his whole life. Both of his sisters had married hockey players—guys who were always among the elite players in the league, some of the best in the world at their positions.

He was surrounded by people who had what he wanted. If I were in his position, I'd probably be jealous as hell of everyone I encountered. But even if there was a bit of jealousy lurking in him, that wasn't what shone through for me.

What I saw was his determination. His drive. His desire to make his father proud. His need to make his own mark on the world, in whatever manner he could.

But it was starting to look as if that mark would have to be made somewhere other than on the ice. My heart broke for him. And I knew all too well what disappointment of any sort could do to a guy. Mine came from a different side of life, but it was no less prevalent and painful.

I missed seeing him every day now that he couldn't take part in things the way he had been before training camp started. When I went into Starbucks on my way in, I had to stop myself from ordering a coffee for him, since he wouldn't be there. When I stumbled in to find Koz once again doing naked yoga in the middle of the room, Luke was the first person I thought of, because I knew he'd have a similar response to mine.

But he was at home or out pounding the pavement looking for a job or God only knew where—except he wasn't here.

When we had a post-practice scrimmage and everyone played out of position, I couldn't help but think about Luke's attempts at taking face-offs as I watched guys like 501 attempt to do the same. Was he still practicing them? Had he found some other hockey players to skate with while they waited for news from their agents?

Every time I pulled out my phone and thought about sending him a text or dialing his number, I had to force myself to stop. It was one thing to be friendly with him as long as he was reciprocating; it was something else entirely to pursue him—especially since I'd promised myself I wouldn't get involved in a relationship until I'd retired.

And maybe Luke didn't want to be pursued, anyway. He could call me just as easily, but he hadn't done anything of the sort. Maybe that was my sign, and I needed to heed it.

After a hard skate one day, less than a week into training camp, I was sitting in my stall, removing my skates, when Anne Golston came in carrying a video camera herself. Usually, she wasn't the one behind the lens, which was why I paused and took notice. She was the producer, but she had a crew of cameramen who did most of the filming while she told them what she wanted filmed.

I was so surprised by this turn of events that I sat up and listened.

She walked over to Riley Jezek's stall, the camera under an arm, resting on her hip.

"Short staffed?" RJ asked.

"Had three guys leave in the off-season for other projects. Still haven't found a replacement for them yet." She didn't seem overly concerned, though. Something told me Anne liked being hands-on when it came to her work. "Nate tells me you're planning to take Phoebe swimming with Max and Lola later," she said.

Phoebe was RJ's kitten; Max and Lola were his Mastiffs.

Taking a cat to the pool sounded like a death wish, to me. But that kitten wasn't like most other cats I'd ever been around. She went for walks on a leash with the dogs, so maybe she'd swim, too? No telling. At least not until they tried it out.

RJ grinned. "That's the plan. I don't know how she'll handle it, but we're going to see."

"They're letting you take her to Doggy Paddles?"

"Got special permission. It'll just be us. But don't tell Mackenzie. She can find out after."

"Bad idea," Hammer said.

"I know cats aren't supposed to like water—"

"I mean trying to keep a secret from your wife, smartass," Hammer cut in. "I don't care what you do with the kitten. But Mackenzie'll find out—probably before the webisode airs, even. And when she does…"

"Never screw with a pregnant woman," Burnzie said from across the room. "I mean, yeah, you can screw her. Just don't screw *with* her."

"Unless you have a death wish," Soupy said.

"And frankly," Jonny put in, coming around the corner with a towel wrapped around his waist, still dripping from the showers, "I don't think you've got a death wish. Don't be a dumb ass."

"So maybe I should talk to Mackenzie about it first," RJ said, sounding as if he had no intention of doing anything of the sort.

"Might not be a bad idea," Anne said.

They all kept talking, but I lost my ability to focus on the conversation—because Webs was standing just inside the room, arms crossed over his chest, staring at me. It was the same stare he'd been giving me back when I'd been helping Luke before training camp had started. And this time, I had no earthly idea what the fuck I'd done to earn it.

I finished drying off after my shower, then hastily pulled on my clothes. When I caught Webs's eye again, he jerked his head toward the hall and headed that way.

I followed.

Once we were well away from the guys, he stopped and spun around, glaring at me with his arms crossed.

"What did I do?" I asked, clueless.

"Don't be an asswipe, Colesy."

"I'm not being an— Wait, what?" That was not what I'd been expecting at all. Maybe, if I'd been pursuing Luke, I might have expected it. But I hadn't been. I'd been doing my damnedest to put him out of my mind. Unsuccessfully, maybe, but that was the intention.

The change in Webs's demeanor was so abrupt I nearly got whiplash. What the fuck was he talking about?

"You heard me. Don't be a fucking asswipe," Webs

ground out.

"I haven't done anything—"

"I know you haven't. That's the problem. You haven't fucking done anything, other than drop off the face of the earth as far as my kid's concerned. You two were damned near inseparable for a few weeks, and now that camp has started, you're ignoring him. So stop being a fucking asswipe, Colesy."

"I'm not ig—"

"He's sulking. He's trying to deal with the fact that his dreams have been crushed. He's trying to cope with the idea that he's not going to get to have a career playing hockey, which is the only thing he ever wanted, the only thing he ever thought he'd do with his life. It's not easy—not for anyone in his shoes. He doesn't know what to do with himself, and he's floundering, and you were the one fucking bright spot for him over the last few weeks. But now? Now you might as well be moving on and leaving him behind, too." He started to walk off, but then he stopped and faced me one more time, his eyes flashing fire. "I've seen the way he looks at you. I've been seeing it for years, since well before he told us he was gay. I already knew it, but I wanted to give him the chance to tell us on his own terms. And I've seen the way you look at him. I know how he acts when he's been around you. He's happy. My kid is fucking happy when he's with you, okay? He hasn't had a whole hell of a lot good going on in his life lately. He needs something good. So just don't be an asswipe. Because I swear to God, Colesy—" He stopped, looking more tortured than I'd ever seen him before. "At least have the fucking balls to tell him it's not going to happen if that's the way it's going to be. Don't leave him wondering. Don't be an asswipe."

Then he stalked off down the hall toward the general manager's office, leaving me wondering what the fuck had just happened.

Luke

My phone buzzed with another text message. Probably from Colesy again. He'd sent me no less than half a dozen messages over the last couple of days, but I hadn't been able to work up the nerve to read them, let alone respond to them. Didn't want to know what he had to say. It'd only make my chest ache worse than it already was.

Or at least that was what I told myself.

I rolled over onto my stomach and dragged the pillow over my head to block out all the sound and light in the room. I already felt like life was suffocating me, so this wouldn't be too different.

My phone buzzed again, though, distracting me from my melancholy.

Damn it.

Without looking at the screen, I pressed and held the button to power off my phone, then tossed it under the blankets.

Not even two minutes later, Dani came barging into my room without bothering to knock first. She ripped the pillow out of my hands and tossed it to the other side of the room. "Enough," she bit off, tugging at my leg. "Get up. Come on. We've got to go downstairs for Jamie and Katie's big announcement."

"What big announcement?" I mumbled, wishing I still had my pillow—because maybe I could use it to muffle my sister's voice. I'd tried it once when we were kids. Hadn't worked then, but it might work now.

It was worth a shot.

She huffed at me, sending her hair flying. "If I knew that, there wouldn't be any need for us to all go out back, now would there?"

"I don't want to hear any announcements." Especially not if it was that my older sister was finally pregnant. Yeah, I wanted her to be happy. But I could only take so much of my sisters' happiness while I was wallowing in my own misery. It only made me feel worse about myself and my predicament, which then made me feel like a shitty brother.

"Too bad," a deep, masculine voice said, surprising me enough that I rolled over to see who else had joined Dani in tormenting me.

Jonny was standing in the open doorway to my bedroom, his arms crossed in front of him in an intimidating pose.

What the hell? "Why're *you* here?" I demanded.

"Hell if I know," he said. "But you're wasting all of our time. They're not going to get started until everyone's present. So get your ass out of bed and come down."

"Who's everyone?" I asked.

"You know," Dani said, sounding miffed, "you really ought to read your text messages once in a while."

"I'm heading down," Jonny said. "If you're not out back with the rest of us in two minutes, I'm going to bring Harry, and we'll drag you." Then he headed into the hall, and I heard his lumbering footsteps going down the stairs.

"You'll be lucky if they just toss you over their

shoulders or something. Cody threatened to string you up by... Well, never mind that. The point is, you'd better get over yourself and come down."

Still sulking, I sat up. "Who else is here?"

"Mom and Dad, of course, Jamie and Katie, me and Cody, Levi and Cadence, and Jonny, Sara, and their kids. Oh, and Sara's dad. And Cody's sisters, since they flew in for a long family visit and the home opener and whatnot. A couple of Jamie and Levi's other brothers are here, too, and his parents. And—"

"Seriously?" I said, cutting her off. What the hell did my sister need that many of us together to say?

"Seriously," Dani said. "Oh, and Ghost and Anne are here, too, along with some of Anne's guys, because Katie and Jamie offered to let them film this for *Eye of the Storm*. So get down there or I *will* get Jonny to carry your ass down. And you can bet I'll enjoy watching it, too."

What the hell did my sister and brother-in-law need all of us together for? And why did they want it filmed? But I supposed the only way I'd find out would be to go down and join the rest of them.

Forcing myself out of bed, I headed for a quick pit stop in the bathroom to splash some water on my face. Then I made my way out back to join the crowd.

I'd barely stepped outside, though, when I came up short and had to fight the urge to book it back inside the house, stat.

Because Cole Paxton was here, too. Convenient how my sister hadn't mentioned him, in the long list of other people she'd mentioned. If she had, I wouldn't have come downstairs at all. I couldn't stand to be around him right now, because he represented everything I wanted but couldn't have.

My stomach lodged itself in my throat when he looked over at me and smiled.

It was all I could do not to turn around and go back upstairs.

Chapter Six

Cole

In so many ways, I felt out of place here amongst the extended Weber family. Yeah, I'd been playing with Babs, Harry, Jonny, and even 501, for a long time now. I'd played a few seasons with Webs before he'd retired and joined the coaching staff. But for the most part, this was a family gathering—extended family, sure, but I didn't qualify under any explanation of that nature.

Ghost and Anne were here because Anne would be filming a segment for *Eye of the Storm*. Their presence made sense, but I honestly wasn't sure how I fit or why they'd dragged me along.

But I was here. And I felt the pain in Luke's gaze, and I knew that I was at least somewhat responsible for it, which made me feel like shit.

He dragged a lawn chair away from where it'd

initially been positioned, plopping down in the seat once it was just far enough away to give him some space but not so far that anyone would think he was trying to distance himself.

I knew better, though. And I was almost positive that his sisters and parents, at the very least, did, too, even if he could hide it from the majority of the people present.

Before I could second-guess myself, I took my lawn chair and positioned it directly next to his.

His head shot up and he glared daggers at me, but he didn't get a chance to bite my head off before Babs and Katie were standing in front of everyone, the cameras were rolling, and his opportunity was gone—unless he wanted to make a scene.

I didn't get the impression that Luke wanted to do anything of the sort. He might want a piece of the spotlight for himself, but he was good at letting others have their moments. He wouldn't want to take anything away from Katie.

"We wanted to bring everyone together tonight for a big announcement," Babs said, and everyone quieted down.

Except for Laura Weber. "Are you pregnant?" she asked her eldest daughter, sounding both excited and nervous all at once.

"No," Katie said. "That's the thing. We've decided to stop trying."

"It's too hard on Katie," Babs said. "All the fertility treatments and miscarriages and whatnot. I can't stand seeing her disappointment anymore."

"It's too hard on *both* of us," she added.

I shot a quick glance over at Luke to see how he was taking this news. His hands were clenched at his sides, his brows drawn together. Katie's struggle with infertility was well known through the team, even though no one really talked about it. We figured it was their business to bring up or not. But it had to have been hard for Luke to watch all this time. Even now, he looked ready to cross over and wrap his sister up in a hug—which, to be honest, was all any of us could do.

"So we're not going to try any longer," Babs said.

Laura Weber did her best to stifle a sob.

Katie smiled at her mother. "It's okay, though. Really, Mom."

"Really?" Laura replied.

"Really," Babs said. "Because we've decided to start the process to become foster parents. Actually, we've already gone through all the initial legwork. We should have our first foster kids soon—maybe later this month, even."

"You're going to adopt?" Just like that, Laura's demeanor shifted.

"Not necessarily," Babs said. "Or at least not right away. We're going to start out as a family for kids who might end up going back to their parents—kids who need a temporary place to stay."

"But depending on the kid and the situation, it might become permanent," Katie said. "We'll just have to see how things pan out."

"Whether we end up adopting or not, though," Babs added, "we're going to need help from all of you. We want to make our home into their home, to give them a family—not just parents but grandparents, aunts and uncles, and cousins. We want this to be as normal as possible for these kids, because it might be the only chance they have of having a normal childhood. We want to be that for them."

"And what happens if you end up pregnant?" Laura asked.

"I'm not going to end up pregnant," Katie said. "Not without some sort of divine intervention. I'm done with fertility treatments and all. I just can't go through that anymore."

"*We* can't," Jamie added. "So we're done with trying. We're going to try to be foster parents. That's the plan. Katie and I have a lot of love to give, and there are a lot of kids out there who need love. We can give it to them—with your help."

The conversation veered off into other things after their pronouncement. Anne's cameramen started moving around, filming conversations among smaller groups. I noticed that Anne didn't seem busy, though, and I had an idea.

"Come with me," I said to Luke.

"I don't want to come with you."

"Shut up and come on. You don't even know what I've got planned." And to be honest, my plan wasn't fully formed. It was more of a fledgling idea, only partially coherent, sure to be haphazard in execution. But arguing with Luke wouldn't help me cement my thoughts.

He didn't get up, though.

"Do you want me to get Jonny to drag you?" I asked.

"Why's everyone threatening me with Jonny all of a sudden?"

"Because everyone knows I can make you do it," Jonny said from behind us, and I had to force myself not to burst out laughing.

Glowering, Luke got up to come with me, and I gave Jonny a quick nod of thanks over my shoulder.

"Where are we going?" Luke demanded.

"You'll find out soon enough."

Anne had separated herself from the group for a moment and was eyeing the crowd, keenly observing everything going on. The thought of what must be going on inside her head at all times was enough to make me dizzy, but she knew what she wanted and how to get it.

When we reached her, I said, "You have a minute?"

"Hmm?" She looked up at me, seeming distracted, but then she blinked and focused in. "Hey. What's up?"

"A couple of days ago, you said you were short staffed. Have you found anyone to fill the holes on your team yet?"

"No, and it's driving me insane. Well, really, it's driving Nate insane. He doesn't like how many hours I'm working these days." She gave me a wry smile.

"For some reason, I get the sense that you *love* working those long hours."

Anne laughed, and her dark eyes lit up. "Busted. But he's right. I can't keep it up like this for too long. Eventually, we're all going to be dealing with burnout."

Luke gave me an annoyed look, and I could tell he was about to bolt, so I reached out a hand to stop him, gently taking hold of his elbow. He jumped at my touch. Hell, I nearly jumped, too, because I wanted to do a hell of a lot more than grab hold of his elbow.

Still, it did the trick—he stayed put.

"So what kind of experience do you need for your team?" I asked, trying to keep it casual even though it was anything but.

"Honestly, not a ton. My guys and I are pretty hands-on. We like things done a certain way. I'd personally train anyone who joins us because I don't want to take any chances and miss the opportunity to get exactly the footage I need. We only get one shot in this business." She narrowed her eyes. "Why? You know someone?"

"Yeah, I know someone," I said. Then I nudged Luke in the ribs. "What about this guy? He's got a degree in journalism. He knows all the ins and outs of the hockey world. He's got great connections in the organization, so he might even be able to get you involved in things you never would have dreamed of before... Maybe not, since you're married to Ghost and all, but you never know. Oh, and he needs a job."

The more I talked, the brighter Anne's eyes got. She gave me a toothy grin. "Brilliant. Absolutely brilliant."

But the glare Luke turned on me was enough to melt an ice sculpture. Good thing I wasn't in any danger of melting. Maybe he was pissed at me now, but he'd probably thank me for it later.

"Come sit and talk with me," Anne said, hooking her arm with Luke's and hauling him off to a couple of empty chairs near the house, well away from the crowd, giving them a bit of privacy.

Even though I was tempted to follow them, I didn't. I'd helped open the door, but Luke was the one who'd have to walk through it. I headed over to the picnic tables the Webers had set up, piled high with barbecue chicken, burgers, and steaks that Jonny was grilling, as well as countless sides and desserts. As I fixed myself a plate, I felt someone come up behind me.

"That's a start," Webs said quietly, but it was a menacing sort of quiet tone he'd used. "You're working on getting yourself out of asswipe territory. But you still need to do better, Colesy."

"I'm working on it," I muttered. But I could only deal with one thing at a time. And I couldn't very well do *anything* if the guy wouldn't respond to my texts or phone calls. I wasn't going to become a stalker just to appease David Weber.

"Work harder," he ground out.

Yeah. Work harder. I planned to…and I wasn't finished tonight.

I just didn't have a clue what the next step needed to be.

Taking my plate to sit with Jonny, Sara, and their kids, I kept a close eye on Luke. Maybe I'd see something that would lead me in the right direction. Maybe he'd give me some clue. That was the hope, at least. I focused on my food and tried not to draw attention to the fact that I was overly interested in the conversation taking place on the other side of the lawn.

At least Luke hadn't stalked off, though. He and Anne were in deep discussion, their heads close together.

He used his hands when he spoke—or at least he did when he was fully engaged in the topic—and after a few minutes, I started to notice him gesticulating quite a bit. His hands were even more expressive than his face.

Good. Maybe my plan—fledgling and not at all well-thought-out though it might be—wouldn't backfire on me, after all.

Luke

"Can you come up to my office in the morning?" Anne asked, looking more relaxed than she had all night—maybe even relieved. "I'll need you to fill out some employment paperwork before you can officially get started, but I'd love to have you training by later in the week. I can have you working alongside Ben for the first preseason game."

"Yeah, sure," I said, my mind still reeling.

"I can't tell you how excited I am about this!" she said. "I mean, my guys are awesome, don't get me wrong, but none of them have ever played hockey. And even though Nate helps me with a lot of that stuff..." She shook her head. "You'll give us a whole new perspective on the team and the game. This is going to be great."

"Great," I repeated, because I couldn't think of anything else to say.

Anne practically bounced out of her chair and wrapped me up in a hug. When she pulled away, she said, "Sorry. Got carried away. But this is the best thing ever, Luke."

"No, it's…" The word *fine* died on my tongue, because she had already bustled off to whisper something in the ear of one of her crew members.

She'd barely been gone for twenty seconds when Colesy came over, a wary look in his eye, and claimed her seat. I tried to glare at him, because I was still pissed—but I couldn't put much behind it. The truth was, my anger wasn't directed at him. I was just angry with the world. Angry with myself. Angry with all the shit in my life that hadn't gone the way I'd envisioned it going.

But maybe not getting to play pro hockey wasn't the end of the world. Maybe a career didn't have to define me, after all.

"Do I need to apologize?" he asked.

"If you ask Dani, I'm the one who needs to apologize."

"Not to me, you don't."

"Yeah, I do. I've been sulking like an ass. I'm sorry."

"And I'm sorry for dropping out of your life the way I did."

I shot him a questioning look and shook my head. "You're busy. I get it."

"Not so busy I can't call you sometimes."

"You don't need to call me," I said, my tongue getting stuck in my throat.

"Maybe I want to call you."

"Why would—"

"I miss talking to you," he cut in. "I miss hanging out with you."

"You've already got a lot going on."

"Not so much I can't make an effort to see you."

"If it's something you have to make an effort to do, then maybe you're better off without it." Maybe he was better off without *me*. That was what I'd been thinking for the last few days, anyway.

But he pinned me with a stare that made me think all sorts of things I shouldn't be thinking right now. Made me want things I shouldn't want. I wanted him to look at me that way when he had me pinned against the wall, when he was about to kiss the shit out of me, but that couldn't be happening.

Could it?

"Knock it off, Luke," he said, and his voice had gone husky and growly.

I licked my lips, staring down at my lap because I couldn't look in his eyes any longer without having my boner pop up and make things awkward. But it was too late—I was already sporting wood, and I didn't think I'd be able to hide it. "So what are you saying?" I finally asked.

"I'm saying I want to spend time with you. I want to hang out with you." He waited until I made the mistake of meeting his heated gaze. "I want to be with you. I didn't want to want it—to want *you*—but I do. I thought I'd wait until I retired to get involved with someone. But then again, I didn't intend to come out until after I'd retired, and that's already been blown out of the water."

"You want…" I couldn't even finish the thought, couldn't wrap my brain around it.

There had to be a punch line coming, a *haha gotcha* moment. Something.

But he looked me straight in the eye, and he said, "To be with you, yeah," and no laughter followed.

The cameras were all the way across the yard, focusing on my parents and my sisters and their husbands. Everyone else was eating, talking, and generally having a good time, oblivious to the seriousness of our conversation, completely unaware that my heart was on the verge of either filling so full it would burst or shattering into a million pieces.

"That's why I've been trying to help you out so much," he said. "Because I care. Maybe I care too much. Maybe if I get involved with you, I won't be doing the best thing for my career. Maybe this'll blow up into a huge media circus and I'll wish I'd never said a fucking word—"

"You won't wish that," I cut in.

He cocked up a brow. "You sure about that? I'm not like you, Luke. I don't want to blaze any trails. I don't want to bust in doors and knock down walls for other people in my shoes. I just want to do my job and go home to lead a quiet life where no one cares if I'm gay or not. But now, every cable sports program wants to do a feature on me. Every sports magazine wants an interview. Every city we go to, the radio shows want to do a segment on me. Every time I turn around, my agent is hitting me up with another *offer,* but it's not what I want."

I might not want to admit it, but there was an awful lot of truth in what he was implying about what I'd wanted. It wasn't just the career, although that was a big part of it. I'd wanted to be the one breaking down those barriers for other guys like me and Colesy so that it'd be easier for the next guy to come out.

But that wasn't a mantle anyone should have to carry unless he wanted it. I did; Colesy didn't.

"Looks like you've got what I want and I've got what you want," I said.

"Sure seems that way, doesn't it?"

"So now what?" I asked. Because if we got involved with each other, he was the one in the spotlight, not me. I'd just be the sidekick, the non-famous partner, not the one having to deal with all the features and interviews.

It was a lot to ask of someone who didn't want anything to do with the firestorm that was sure to follow.

He glanced around my parents' backyard, taking stock and lost in his own thoughts. I followed his gaze. My parents were in deep discussion with Jamie and Katie. The other guys from the team and their wives and kids were eating, talking, laughing…except for Jonny, who was still manning the grill. Anne and her crew were spread out, but none of them were near the two of us.

It seemed everyone had decided to give us some privacy.

When Colesy faced me again, his eyes were blazing. "Wanna get out of here? I think we can get away with sneaking out now."

My heartbeat was so frantic I thought my heart might explode inside the walls of my chest. But I licked my lips, and I said, "Yeah. Let's go."

Chapter Seven

Luke

I didn't know where Colesy was taking me, and to be honest, I didn't quite care. I just wanted to be with him, somewhere we could be well away from all the prying eyes in my parents' backyard, not to mention away from the cameras. I didn't mind being the poster boy for gay hockey players, in terms of helping them find the courage to come out, but this was different. It was private, or at least it should be.

Whatever this thing between us might become, I didn't want it to play out on *Eye of the Storm*. It felt too personal for that. Too intimate. This wasn't something the whole world needed to witness. Maybe the aftermath, sure. Maybe we wouldn't just be the first two openly gay hockey players, but we might be the first openly gay couple in the broader hockey world.

But this part, the early stages? No one needed to be involved but the two of us. Especially not until we figured out what we wanted it to be. I knew what I wanted, but Colesy? He was still a mystery to me. Whatever this relationship would become, we needed to figure it out ourselves before it became a *thing*.

Besides, if I was now going to be working behind the cameras on *Eye of the Storm*, then I didn't need to be on screen any more than necessary. I intended to take a page from Anne's book in that regard, keeping the focus on the people involved with the team and not on me.

Colesy didn't seem inclined to talk much now that we were in the car and away from prying eyes, so I took a cue from him. But without talking to calm me down, my nerves started running away with me. I'd fooled around with a couple of guys back in college. Well, first I'd fooled around with girls, trying to convince my mind and body to cooperate, to convince myself that I was straight and not gay. It hadn't worked out too well. Still, though…experimenting—that was what college kids were supposed to do, right?

None of it had ever been with someone I actually cared about, though. It hadn't ever meant anything. It hadn't ever felt like more than a college kid trying to get his rocks off.

This? This would mean something. At least to me, it would.

And that had me more than just a little anxious.

Before long, we were in the Hawthorne District, and then he was pulling into the private garage at a swanky condo near the Baghdad Theater, and my tongue felt like it might lodge in my throat.

"You don't need to be nervous," Colesy said,

breaking the silence so suddenly that it startled me. "I'm not planning to throw you against the wall and have my way with you just yet."

"I'm not…" But I didn't want to lie to him, so I cut myself off before denying the truth. I was nervous as hell. Besides, I kind of liked the thought of him throwing me against the wall and having his way with me. I'd been imagining variations of that for years, and maybe some of the reverse, too. But I preferred the thought of him manhandling me. Maybe. Gah, I couldn't be sure.

And now, I doubted I'd be able to stop thinking about that very thing until he did it. He climbed out and headed inside, and I followed.

Once we were in his place, he cocked a grin in my direction, and my heart tripped up. "You're nervous," he said. "It's okay. So am I."

"Why're you nervous?"

The brow over his right eye shot up above his sandy-brown hairline. "Why am I nervous? Are you even serious right now? It's not every day I bring someone home with me."

"You don't…" I shrugged, hoping he could fill in the blanks on his own.

My eyes started wandering, almost of their own volition, taking in his place. The furniture and décor were simple—straight lines, neutral tones, nothing splashy or flashy. An abstract painting above the fireplace had a bold splash of bright red, but that was almost the only bit of non-neutral color in the entire room. He had a bit of tasteful, modern art on the walls, and a large, clear vase of white calla lilies on the coffee table in the living room.

It was open concept, so I had a clear view of the

kitchen and dining room, too. Nothing was out of place. He had stainless steel appliances and a rack of pots and pans hanging above the kitchen island. It was spotless, but everything looked well-used.

Did that mean he liked to cook? And would he cook for me, someday?

An image of the two of us getting up together on a lazy weekend morning and making breakfast flashed through my mind, but I did my best to banish it before it took root. Better not to get ahead of myself.

The whole place was clean and pristine, much like the man himself. For some reason, seeing that it wasn't decked out in gaudy, garish colors or full of black leather and whatnot helped me relax.

When I faced him again, his lips quirked up in a halfhearted grin. "I spent the first decade plus of my career fully closeted, or as close as I could get, Luke. I didn't want to be a torch bearer, so I did everything I could to keep it a secret. My private life is no one else's business, you know? Burnzie knew. Maybe a few of the other boys, too—but if they did, they never said anything about it. They respected my privacy, my right to come out on my own terms, if I even wanted to do it at all. But I sure as fuck haven't been bringing guys home with me or going home with them. Too many possibilities for word to get out when I wasn't ready for it to get out." He shrugged, heading into the kitchen. When he came back, he had two beers in his hands. He passed one to me. "But now everything's out in the open, so I guess there's no point in trying to step back into the closet. Not sure I'd want to, anyway. It's a lot nicer being able to be myself."

For some reason, that made my pulse go haywire. Maybe because of the potential implications.

I opened my beer and took what I intended to be a sip, but it was actually a massive swallow that nearly choked me.

Colesy was *out*, but he hadn't ever been in a relationship that was public knowledge. If he had been, he was absolutely, one hundred percent right. It would have been all over social media, and maybe even the mainstream hockey media. As the first openly gay player in the NHL, his relationship status would be major news, even though it ought to be private if he wanted it to be. Was that what he meant?

He headed into the living room and took a seat on the couch. It looked sleek and uncomfortable, like a piece of furniture meant to be looked at more than lived in. I sat next to him—close enough to touch him if I wanted, but not quite touching. Surprisingly, I was able to sink into it and relax. It was a lot more comfortable than it appeared.

And I *did* want to touch him. I wanted to do a hell of a lot more than that, too. But I wasn't sure when or how to make my move.

The guys I'd fooled around with in college hadn't been like Colesy. They'd been young and inexperienced and dumb, much like me. But he was…different. Older, yeah, but that wasn't the only thing. He was so sure of himself, of who he was and what he wanted out of life. He wasn't experimenting or trying to figure things out still. He knew what he wanted, and that was hot as fuck.

"So you'd be open to the idea of having the world know you were involved with someone now?" I asked cautiously. "Is that what you're saying?"

"I still don't think it's anyone's business but my own." He took a swig of his beer, eyeing me over the top of the bottle. "But I don't suppose it'd be too different from any of the other guys. The whole world knows Babs and Katie are together. The same with Harry and Dani, and Jonny and Sara, and every other guy on the team who's married or in a serious relationship, and every guy on every other team in the league. It's how things work when you play pro sports these days, apparently. Don't see why the world would treat my relationship any differently."

"There might be more focus on you than there is on them," I pointed out. Not that I wanted him to reconsider what he was apparently considering. But it was only fair for him to consider all of the potential ramifications. "I mean, this could be bigger than Jamie-and-Katie-level uber-fandom at the height of her popularity. It could even reach Mike Fisher and Carrie Underwood status, or Ray and Viktoriya Chambers. Although with those two, I suppose it'd be more notoriety than fandom."

He cracked a grin and made my heart melt a bit. "You think a gay couple will cause a bigger stir than a hockey player marrying a porn star?"

"Maybe." I shrugged.

"Yeah, maybe. Or maybe it won't." He took another sip of his beer, then set the bottle on the coffee table, carefully situating it on a coaster. When he met my eyes again, there was a determined crease to his brow that fascinated me. "Maybe it'll die off once the next big scandal hits. Maybe no one'll care once someone else does something more audacious than daring to be true to himself."

"I like you pretty well just the way you are," I said.

"Too bad there aren't more people in the world like you."

"There are. There are a lot of people out there who don't give a shit who someone goes home with at the end of the day."

"And it seems like sometimes there are just as many who're determined to tear you down if you aren't who *they* want you to be."

"Your family?" I asked tentatively.

"I might as well be dead to them."

"You've got a family here."

"Teammates, sure. Friends. But not family."

"Maybe they're not your blood family, but they can be the family you choose. Sometimes, that's more important anyway."

"What would you know about that?" Colesy asked, giving me a wry smile and smothering a laugh. "You've got an amazing family."

"I have an obnoxious family."

"An obnoxious family full of people who love you no matter what. Don't ever forget that. Maybe they piss you off sometimes, but they love you."

"I'm sure your family—"

But whatever I was about to say about his family died on my lips, because he cut me off with the hottest kiss I'd ever experienced in my life. He trapped my face between both of his hands, angling my head toward his, and then leaning into me so much that I fell back against the cushions, pulling him along with me. His tongue pressed against the seam of my lips, so I opened and let him in. Then I wanted to drown in the taste of him, to lose myself in the bossy way he grabbed my head and held me how he wanted me.

Beer? Who needed beer?

I could get drunk on kissing Cole Paxton.

Cole

Kissing the hell out of Luke Weber was a lot fucking better than thinking or talking about my family. I should've done it as soon as we'd walked into my place, shoved him up against the wall like I'd mentioned earlier instead of trying to ease his nerves with conversation.

It would've been better for both of us, most likely.

The path I'd taken had only served to piss me off, because I didn't want to even *think* about my father, let alone talk about him. And trying to talk first had allowed Luke's anxiety to get the better of him, so now I had to help relieve his anxiety as well as my own frustrations.

But kissing Luke? That was something I could get on board with. It was exactly what I needed. And it seemed to be what he needed, too, based on the way he was responding.

His beer forgotten, he growled against my lips and grabbed hold of my biceps with both hands, tugging me closer until I was practically on top of him. I leaned in farther, angling him back against the couch so he'd have something to brace himself with, and split his lips with my tongue.

He let out a happy, strangled sound, if there could be such a thing, and slid his tongue alongside mine.

His *pierced* tongue.

Holy hell. How the fuck had I never noticed that before? I was already sporting some serious wood, but that discovery made my boner get a boner. I reached down to adjust myself, but then I wished I hadn't, because now my dick was practically begging for more attention than that brief touch.

It wasn't enough. I needed more. Couldn't get close enough, no matter how hard I tried—not in this position, side by side.

I hitched myself up on my knees and straddled him, pushing him back against the cushions of the couch. Luke didn't seem to mind—in fact, he wrapped his arms around my back and tugged me closer until I was virtually draped across his lean, hard body.

He was a lot stronger than he looked, not that the realization surprised me. I'd been on the ice with him enough over the last few weeks. I knew at least *some* of what he could do with that body.

But now I wanted to find out more.

Luke seemed to have the same idea. Before I could do anything about it, he was already tugging at the buckle of my belt and trying to get my shirt free at the same time. I lifted my shirt up and over my head, tossing it to the floor while he ripped my belt free from the loops and lost it somewhere.

I reached in to strip off his shirt, too, but he was already kissing a path down my chest and using a pointed tongue to swirl around my nipple and then placing wet, openmouthed kisses on my flesh. His piercing flicked over my sensitive skin, completely stealing my train of thought. He closed his lips over me and added suction, and I shuddered.

He shifted a hand down to my dick and rubbed me over my jeans, not that I needed any extra friction. Oh, hell. It'd been ages since this kind of heat had consumed me.

"I want to suck you off," he said, his voice rough

and raspy in between kisses. He lifted needy eyes up to meet mine.

Holy shit.

I wasn't sure what I'd been planning when I brought Luke to my place, but it wasn't this. Maybe a bit of making out. Maybe some heavy petting. Something like that would have been nice even if I wasn't *expecting* it. Maybe just beers and talking, though. I would've been okay with that, too.

I'd never made a habit of jumping straight into sex. At least not when it was someone who mattered to me. I'd had meaningless hookups with men before, even with Burnzie's brother once, several years ago. I was cautious about who I hooked up with, of course. I needed to trust them enough to know word wouldn't get out, that they'd keep my secrets safe.

But what I'd had with those guys had never been about anything more than sex, nothing but scratching an itch that we both needed scratched.

I'd done everything possible to avoid getting truly involved with someone because I wanted my secret to stay a secret until I was ready for it to be public knowledge.

But now? It wasn't a secret any longer. The closet door had closed behind me months ago, and I couldn't go back to the other side of it even if I wanted to. Which I didn't.

I had no intention for this thing with Luke to be about nothing other than sex. I wanted it to be something more. Something bigger. I wanted it to have meaning.

What that meaning might be, exactly, I wasn't sure yet, but I didn't think either of us were capable of treating this like a random hookup, a quick blow job, or maybe even something slightly more than a blow job.

This felt like the beginnings of a real relationship—and that was a thought that shook me to my core. A long time ago, I'd given up all hope of having a relationship like this until I was no longer playing pro hockey. It shook me almost as much as the things Luke was doing to me with his hands and kisses and tongue.

A groan tore through my chest when his deft fingers moved to my fly. He had me unzipped and free before I could register that he meant what he'd said, and then strong fingers circled my aching cock.

He stroked me a few times, tugging just hard enough but not too hard.

"Fuck, Luke. You're killing me."

"Don't even have my mouth on you yet." He shot me a wicked grin. "You don't know how long I've been thinking about this—how long I've wanted you."

I debated asking him how long, but he took me into his mouth before I could get another word out. Then all I could do was try not to come too soon—which wasn't easy, since it'd been way too long since my poor, deprived dick had seen any action other than my own hand.

Add that tongue ring to the mix, and I'd be lucky to last two minutes.

He pumped me with one hand, his other braced on my thigh to keep me from falling over backward. Which turned out to be a good thing, because after a couple of swirls of his tongue and a long, hard draw, my head fell back, and the rest of me would've followed suit, otherwise.

His tongue was wicked. And his piercing was almost more than I could take. The hard ball felt almost cool in contrast to the soft, wet heat of his tongue and lips. He took long, deep drags of me. I dug my fingers into his shoulders, desperate for something to hold on to; he did the same with my thighs. The pinch of pain was just enough to keep me from falling off the couch in ecstasy. Instead, I pumped my hips in time with his strokes.

And then he moved a hand back to my crease. His finger found my hole.

When he started massaging my prostate, though? Game over. As hot as I already was, and as long as it had been for me, there wasn't any chance of holding back the intensity of my climax. I didn't even have time to warn him that I was coming, unless you counted tensing up and shouting something frantic and garbled that I couldn't even understand, myself—but by then, it was too late, anyway.

Luke didn't seem phased in the least. If anything, he had a cocky sort of grin on his face as he licked his lips and sucked my already softening cock with another long draw. "That was so fucking hot," he said.

So fucking hot? That didn't even begin to cover it.

I was in trouble.

Because now that I'd had a taste, I'd never have enough.

Chapter Eight

Luke

Somehow, I'd gone from the lowest of low points in my life to the highest of highs, all within the span of a few days. Or…as close as I could get to the high point, since I wasn't playing pro hockey anywhere. Still, despite my failure in that department, things were looking pretty damn good.

Anne Golston and the *Eye of the Storm* team were a hell of a lot of fun to work with, and doing this sort of documentary work was turning out to be not only challenging but stimulating. Even though I'd only gotten my degree in journalism because I'd needed to be working toward a degree to play hockey in college, I'd been smart enough to choose a field I liked. Finding ways to use what I'd learned in school and to combine it with what I'd spent my life doing on the ice was both rewarding and motivating.

Plus, it meant I got to spend more time hanging out with Colesy and the rest of the guys. Yeah, I had to keep a bit of distance from him when I was behind the lens, metaphorically if not physically, but when I was off duty, things were different.

Trading blow jobs with Colesy just about every night certainly didn't hurt my disposition any, either. And since I was working as part of the *Eye of the Storm* crew, that meant I got to travel with the team when they went on the road. We were on the plane with the guys. We were at the various arenas with them. We were in the same hotel as them… It was a hell of a lot easier on me to sneak into his room on the road than it was to wonder if my mother or sisters would be spying on me in Portland.

Mom probably wouldn't do that, to be honest. And Katie had much more important things on her mind these days than worrying about who her little brother might or might not be screwing. But Dani? Dani was meddlesome like nobody's business—even more so now that she was pregnant. She was constantly sticking her nose where it didn't belong, and I wasn't ready to involve my family in whatever this might become.

Dad, at least, had the decency to stay out of my private life. I mean, I knew if there was something I needed to talk to him about, he'd be open to it—even something he had no experience with. But he wasn't interfering in things, as far as I was aware.

Colesy was old enough and had been in the league for long enough that he didn't have a road roommate. He got a room to himself, which meant we had plenty of privacy to do whatever the hell we wanted.

We were in St. Louis tonight.

The Storm beat the Blues in a shootout, and after a brief team breakfast tomorrow morning, we'd all be getting on a plane and flying to Minnesota.

Colesy'd had an average night—no goals or assists himself, but the Blues hadn't scored while he and Hammer had been on the ice, either. For a couple of older, third-pairing, stay-at-home defensemen in this league, that was exactly what he wanted to see on his stat sheet after a game—a big slew of zeroes. That meant he and Hammer had done their jobs well.

But now the game was over, we were all back at the hotel, and the *Eye of the Storm* crew was calling it a night.

Anne caught me sneaking down the halls of the hotel to join Colesy, but since she was on her way to Ghost's room herself, she didn't say anything. She just gave me a grin and a wink and then let me slip wordlessly past her.

I turned the corner and almost bumped straight into my father, who was on his way back toward the elevators.

He gave me a funny look, raising an eyebrow in question. "Thought your room was on the sixth floor."

We were currently on the eleventh floor of the hotel.

"I was just…" Scrambling to come up with something to say to my old man. How do you tell your father you're on your way to a booty call with one of his players?

Just then, Colesy, Hammer, Nicky, and Leif Sorenson came around the corner, talking and laughing. They each had a to-go bag from a nearby restaurant in their hands.

Dad turned toward them and said, "Hmm," under his breath when Colesy looked over at us and smiled so wide it made my heart stop.

Hmm? What did that mean?

Colesy separated himself from the other guys. Those three headed into a room in the corner after a brief wave hello, and he made his way toward us.

"Hungry?" he asked me, totally at ease, as if my father wasn't glaring straight through him. "I've got plenty."

I felt hungry, all right, but not for food. But I nodded and said, "Yeah, I could eat."

Dad scowled at me, and I shrugged. Then he glared at Colesy one more time and stalked off down the hall.

"What was that about?" I asked once my father had gone around the corner.

"He's your father," he said, laughing.

"Yeah, but still." I didn't know what to make of it. Didn't know what Colesy made of it, either. He tended to keep his thoughts to himself about a lot of things, whereas I was an open book.

He fished his key card out of his pocket and shrugged. "Just his way of telling me not to be an asswipe or something. Only he's already told me that before, and it was for a completely different reason."

Wait, what? "My dad's told you not to be an asswipe?" Something fluttered in the pit of my stomach.

"Yeah. Sort of." Colesy's expression was sheepish. "A few times, even," he added dryly.

Maybe my father wasn't keeping his nose out of my private life as well as I'd thought, after all. "Meaning what?"

"It's kind of what he does when someone's pursuing one of his kids. In case you hadn't noticed."

A tingle of awareness shot straight up my spine at

the idea that Cole Paxton was admitting he was pursuing me—at least in a roundabout way. "I've noticed," I said, swallowing the lump in my throat. Dad had been awful with both Babs and Harry back in the day. "But still. I'm not one of his daughters. It's different for me."

"You think?"

"Isn't it?" I'd never been one of Dad's little girls. Thank goodness for that.

Cole winked. "It just means he loves his kids—all of you—and he wants the best for you. That's all."

Something told me he wasn't telling me the full story. "Does that mean he doesn't think you're what's best for me?"

"Give your father some credit, Luke. He trusts you to know your own mind. Besides, it's nice that you have parents who give a shit who you want to be with." He headed into the room and set the to-go bag down on the desk, then started taking out all the food he'd brought back with him from the restaurant, effectively putting an end to that line of discussion.

The bag wasn't just filled with leftovers from his dinner, either. He'd ordered an entire meal for me, apparently, since the to-go container he set in front of me was completely untouched: half a roast chicken, steamed Brussels sprouts with some sort of garlicky balsamic glaze, and decadent mashed potatoes with truffle oil.

He took out another, smaller container and started eating his dessert—German chocolate cake with traditional coconut pecan frosting.

I raised a brow. "Should you be eating that?" Most hockey players tended to eat a relatively strict diet during the season. Sugary desserts weren't high on the list of acceptable foods.

"Nope." He cocked a sexy-as-hell grin at me. "But I'm a sucker for German chocolate. It's my biggest weakness."

Dessert was good, but I'd never go so far as to say anything of the sort was my biggest weakness. *He* was my biggest weakness.

"There's dessert in the bag for you, too. Lemon cheesecake."

Oh my god. My mouth started watering at the thought. "I might die and go to heaven." Okay, so maybe I should put a qualifier on that earlier thought. Lemon cheesecake and Colesy were my biggest weaknesses. Not necessarily in that order.

But now I was thinking about putting my lemon cheesecake on him and then licking every bit of that tart, creamy goodness off his body.

"Don't do that or you'll miss out on a lot more lemon cheesecake," he said, which made me do a double take. But he didn't know what I was thinking about doing to him. I needed to slow my roll. He laughed and winked. "Babs told me lemon cheesecake was your favorite."

I intended to eat my meal like a civilized person and not someone imagining licking my dessert off Cole's hard body. "Jamie was with you guys tonight?" I asked, trying to keep it casual. But what I really wanted to ask him was why he'd bothered to ask my brother-in-law about my favorite dessert. And when he'd done it.

Instead, I stuffed my face with mashed potatoes.

"Nah," he said. "He and 501 were trying to keep Koz in line."

Good luck with that... But I was still baffled. "You bought a whole meal for me?" And he must have asked

Jamie what I liked at some other point in time, then. One more thing to show how thoughtful Colesy was, just like him knowing my coffee order.

Damn, I needed to get better at this shit.

"You've been forgetting to eat lately," he murmured. "You're too much like Anne for your own good, at least in that way. Both of you get caught up in your work and forget about everything else."

There was some truth to that, but I hadn't forgotten about *everything* else. The number one thing on my mind lately had been *him*—when I could see him next, how much I wanted his hands on me, when I should make a move to take things to the next level between us, whether he was as preoccupied with me as I was with him…

If he was making the effort to find out my favorite dessert and bring it to me, though, I supposed that could serve as a reasonable answer to the last bit.

Still… "But you aren't worried that any of those guys might—" I shrugged, cutting myself off and letting him fill in the blanks. Besides, the chicken smelled too good, and he was right. I was starving. My stomach had started making some embarrassing sounds as soon as the scents wafted toward me, and it didn't seem like it would stop until I'd fed the beast. I filled my plastic spork with mashed potato and greedily dug in.

"None of the guys care about that kind of shit, Luke. Not like that. Or if they do, they're smart enough to keep their opinions to themselves, because the rest of the team wouldn't put up with ignorance like that."

"Maybe you're right," I said, but I wasn't sure I believed it. Because even if some of them didn't care, there were also guys like Koz, who made a point of being an asshole at every possible moment.

We both fell silent, me so I could eat, and Colesy because…well, I wasn't sure why he clammed up, exactly. He stared at me, quietly eating his dessert, his gaze full of heat.

The intensity of his attention on me made me hard enough to pound nails. I wanted to forget all about my meal and get straight to what *I* wanted for dessert— him—but I didn't think he'd let me off so easily. So I ate.

After he finished his dessert and cleared away the trash, he slipped into the bathroom for a few minutes. I finished my meal, but I was too full for dessert right now, so I put the cheesecake into the mini-fridge in his room. It'd be a great midnight snack, or maybe even breakfast.

When I turned around again, Cole was coming out of the bathroom in nothing but his boxer-briefs. Hard, rippling muscle covered every inch of him, but my eye was drawn as always to the smattering of light-brown hair disappearing below the waistband of his shorts.

My mouth watered at the sight of his hard bulge. He stroked himself over the fabric, and I nearly came in my pants.

And then I saw what was in his other hand—a foil condom wrapper and a bottle of lube.

Yeah, all that watering from a moment ago? Gone. My mouth was as dry as the Sahara Desert.

"Is this really happening?" I croaked. And then I started to panic, because I hadn't prepared myself at all. Anal wasn't something I could just jump into. It wasn't something *anyone* should just jump into without adequate preparation. That was a bad, bad, bad idea.

Cool as a cucumber, Colesy held out a hand for me

and said, "I want you to fuck me, Luke."

Holy. Fucking. Shit.

Chapter Nine

Cole

"Are you being serious right now?" Luke spluttered, looking shocked and fascinated and seriously turned on all at once.

"Dead serious." I cocked up a brow, suddenly questioning myself.

Maybe I'd misread him. Maybe he wasn't ready to take things further than we already had. In which case, I'd gotten myself into a serious pickle.

"Unless you don't want—"

He groaned. "I want it. Fuck, do I ever want it. I want *you*."

"Good, because I want you, too. And I need you right now. So are you going to get over here and undress for me, or what?"

I sounded bossy and almost frantic, even to my own

ears. But I supposed my impatience in this instance was my own fault. I'd intended to seduce Luke with a meal—wine him and dine him, so to speak, and then let things progress naturally. Until the guys had dragged me into going out to grab a bite with them after the game.

Problem was, I'd already put in a small string of anal beads to prime myself up for tonight. I'd tossed them in my gym bag before the game, and I'd gone into a bathroom stall afterward to discreetly take care of things before we'd left the arena.

Over the years, I'd rarely ever allowed any man to top me—it takes a lot of trust, and frankly, because of my father, I didn't tend to trust many people very much—so I knew I'd need a decent amount of prepping before I could handle it. But I wanted this with Luke, more than I could say, so I thought I'd try to make it easier for both of us.

I shouldn't have gone out with the guys. I should've picked up dinner for me and Luke and come straight back to the hotel, like I'd initially planned. But I was a sucker, apparently, and overly concerned with fitting in as one of the guys—and I'd let them guilt-trip me into coming along with them.

"First road trip of the season," they'd said, tossing in some other shit about team bonding and whatnot. Never mind the fact that most of us had been playing together for years, already, and the guys who were new to the team were being dragged out to dinner with Koz, of all people.

But I'd gone, and by the time we'd gotten back to the hotel, I was ready to come like a motherfucker with nothing more than the slightest provocation. The beads had been caressing my prostate all through dinner, through the walk back to the hotel, through Webs's pseudo-interrogation out in the hallway, and then through watching and waiting for Luke to finish eating. Every step I took had them moving inside me by a tiny degree. Every time I shifted positions while sitting, they rubbed my pleasure center in a new and erotically intense manner.

I'd intended to have them in for thirty minutes or so, maybe an hour at most. This had been closer to three hours.

Yeah, frantic just about summed me up right now. I was ready to explode.

But lucky for me, Luke got up and crossed over to me, a heavy-lidded look to his eyes, and he pushed me against the wall to kiss me, one hand gliding between our bodies to stroke my aching cock over the thin layer of my boxer-briefs. "Fuck, you're hard," he said between kisses.

"Horny as hell," I ground out. Then I dropped to my knees and started ripping at the button and fly of his pants. He was already sporting a semi, but a couple of solid tugs with my hand had him almost as hard as I was.

I circled my tongue around his head before taking him between my lips. He let out a strangled sound from somewhere deep in his chest; I felt the reverberations all the way down to my toes.

"Fuck, that's so good," he said, fisting a hand in my hair and slowing me down.

I didn't want to slow down. I wanted to speed things up because I couldn't wait much longer to have him pounding into me. But I also wanted this to be as good for Luke as I knew it would be for me, so I gave in and forced myself to take my time.

With a pointed tongue, I licked the underside from root to tip, grinning when he stretched up on his toes—whether to get away or to get closer, I wasn't sure.

I took his swollen balls in one hand and gently squeezed.

He let out a strangled sound and pumped his hips slightly faster. "Don't do that too much or I won't last. And I need to get you ready, anyway."

I bobbed over his dick a couple more times and then kissed the leaking tip. "I'm already ready."

His brows quirked up in question, so I stood up, dropped my shorts, and crawled onto my back on the bed. With my knees propped up and my dick bouncing, I kept my gaze trained on Luke.

"Oh my god." His blue eyes were almost black with lust as they zeroed in on the soft handle protruding from my ass. "That's the hottest thing I've ever seen."

"It's about to be the hottest thing you've ever done. Or it will be if you ever get your cute ass over here and fuck me."

That was all the invitation he needed to shuck off the last of his clothes, strewing them all over the floor in his haste. And then he was kneeling between my legs, his hot mouth swallowing my cock as he grasped the ring and slowly—torturously slowly—eased the beads out of me. One at a time, they popped free. Each bead moving past my sphincter caused another thrill of lust to shoot through my body and lodge somewhere near the small of my back.

He worked his tongue ring over the most sensitive parts of my dick, coordinating his movements with the balls slipping past my hole, until I was frantically pumping my hips and desperate to come.

Finally, he had the toy free. I reached for the condom and lube, tossing the foil-wrapped protection in his direction while I took care of the lube myself. By the time I was ready, so was he. Luke took the lube from me and spread some more over the condom. He poured a bit on his hand and rubbed it into me, and then his cockhead was pressing at my hole.

He leaned over me to kiss me, his tongue begging entry just like his cock was. I opened and let him in— in every way. His dick slipped inside almost as easily as his tongue. The fullness and the friction had me moaning into his mouth.

"This is good?" he asked against my lips.

"So fucking good." I rocked my hips up, changing the angle, and then he was moaning almost as much as I was.

Luke braced himself on one elbow and drove into me, jerking my cock with his other hand in time with his strokes.

It was too much. I was too ready, too hot, too needy. "I'm going to come," I said, but it was too late. I was already coming, my jizz shooting all over both of our chests.

Luke gave me a cocky grin just before kissing the hell out of me again. He lifted my legs over his shoulders, adjusting the angle again, and kept pounding into me until he, too, came with a satisfied grunt.

I wrapped my arms and legs around him, trapping him in an embrace, and held on until long after he'd softened and fallen out of me. His breathing slowed, and he rested his head on my chest. I wanted to capture this moment and hold on to it. I wanted to keep it like a framed picture on the mantel, like a home video of blowing out birthday candles, like a perfect, unblemished shell found on the beach and tucked away in a box as a reminder of an untarnished summer.

Because for the first time since I'd told my parents the truth of who I was, I felt loved.

Chapter Ten

Cole

The sun was just starting to stream in through the hotel room's windows when I woke up with Luke's ass nestled against me, my arms wrapped around him, holding him close. His scent surrounded me—warm and spicy, with just a hint of citrus to brighten things up. We'd showered together before going to bed last night, but even though he'd used my toiletries, he still somehow smelled the same way he always did.

I could get used to waking up like this.

My dick liked it, too, if my morning wood was a good indication.

I pressed a kiss to the space where his neck and shoulder met, flicking out my tongue to get a taste of him.

He let out a sound that was somewhere between a yawn and a complaining moan. "It's too early. Sun's barely up."

"Too early for me to kiss you?" I asked, my laughter muffled when I pressed another kiss to the back of his shoulder blade.

"It's never too early for *that*."

"Good." I splayed my hand over his abdomen, dragging him back against me into a tighter fit than before. I liked the feel of his ass pressing against my dick. I *wanted* to get used to this.

He rolled over so we were face-to-face, and he kissed me hard on the lips.

"You keep that up, and something else'll be up, too," I murmured against his lips.

"It already is."

I quirked up a grin. "I suppose so."

"Is that a problem?" He cocked a grin at me, biting his lower lip, his blue eyes full of mischief.

"Since I can't be late for the team breakfast and meeting… Your dad would never let me hear the end of it."

He scowled, but then he planted another quick, hard kiss on me. "You worry too much about my dad."

"With good reason. He's one of my coaches."

"Still… He needs to keep his nose out of my private life."

"He sticks his nose *into* your private life because he cares," I pointed out. "Not everyone has that. Not everyone has parents who give a shit."

"Like you?" he asked solemnly. "That's what you're saying, isn't it?"

I froze.

His hand landed on my biceps, strong and gentle,

stroking as if to comfort me, not to arouse.

"You need to get up," I said. "You should go." Less chance of anyone seeing him sneaking out of my room and back to his own if he went sooner, rather than later. I didn't particularly want to send him on his way just yet, but we had to be sensible about this. And I didn't want to talk about my parents.

But he didn't get up and get moving. He stayed put, staring into my eyes as though he could see through me.

I pecked him on the lips, hoping to cheer him up a bit and make him forget all about my family—or maybe I was just hoping *I* could forget about them. "You need to get back to your own room. Unless you want your father to find you sneaking out of here on his way down to breakfast or something." Or anyone else, for that matter. A lot of people wouldn't give two fucks, but there were plenty more who would.

"He already knows I came to your room last night."

"Yeah, for dinner, not for sex."

"He wasn't born yesterday, you know. I'm sure he can put two and two together."

I reached down and gave Luke a playful pinch on the ass. Then I pushed on his shoulders, urging him out of my bed. "Up. Go. Now."

But he didn't go. Instead, he wrapped his arms tighter around me, holding on with that hidden strength he possessed and refusing to look away. I felt as if he could see all the way inside me, all the things I kept hidden from the world. The tenderness and intensity of his stare made my heart ache.

"You need to go," I repeated, but my voice cracked.

"You keep telling me how good I have it. How great my family is. But you never talk about yours."

I tried to roll away, but Luke wouldn't let me. "There's nothing to talk about," I bit off.

"Bullshit."

"Maybe I don't want to talk about them."

"Maybe I don't want to let you get away with that," he countered.

"They're not like your family."

"Meaning?"

When I didn't immediately respond, he planted a kiss on the tip of my chin, which had to be scratchy with stubble.

I tried to take things further—kissing him full on the mouth. He only let me get away with that for a moment before drawing back and goosing me on the ass.

"What do you mean?" he insisted. "Tell me how your family's different."

"Your parents love you no matter what."

"Yours love you, too. They have to."

"Hmph."

I tried to pull away again, but he wouldn't release me, once again proving he was a hell of a lot stronger than he looked.

"Well, if they love me, they sure have a fucked-up way of showing it."

"Both of them?"

"My father's the worst. My mom just kind of goes along with him. I think she'd be okay with me being gay eventually if not for him. Maybe she wouldn't welcome my lover with open arms or anything, but she wouldn't completely cut me off."

"But he did?"

"Written out of the will and everything," I said wryly.

Luke raised a brow.

"I was a trust-fund baby. My dad's got more money than he knows what to do with. CEO of a big conglomerate. I was supposed to grow up, come along, and take over it for him—after I married an appropriate woman who could act as window dressing, much like my mother did for him. He'd even found the woman for me. She was chosen for the business connections between our two families. He'd arranged how and when I was supposed to propose, and my mother had already started making plans for the wedding. They thought I should just go along with it and be miserable like they were, because that's how things work in families like ours."

"So you told them you wouldn't marry her?"

"Said I wouldn't marry her or any woman because I was gay. And because I wanted to choose my own life and not live the one forced on me by them. I told them I wanted to choose who I would love, but he said there is no such thing as love. That was when I knew I had to leave and follow my own path, no matter what."

"No such thing as love? What a crock of shit."

"I haven't spoken to him since I left to play pro hockey. Used to keep up with my mother. She cut that off, though—last season, when I came out. I called to warn her it would be all over the news and they'd have to deal with it."

"How'd she react?" Luke asked. He'd moved his hands up my arms and was now rubbing my shoulders.

I wanted to melt into his touch.

Instead, I shrugged, effectively brushing his hands away. If only it were as easy to brush my family's hatred away. I'd been trying to dismiss them the way they'd dismissed me for years, but I still hadn't managed it. I still cared.

It hurt, no matter how much I tried to pretend it didn't.

"She spewed a bunch of shit about how selfish of me it was to bring the focus onto myself and my 'abnormalities' when my father's company was in the midst of a huge merger," I said. "She thought the deal might fall through once the other company's CEO got wind of my family's Big Gay Secret. I hung up on her then and haven't spoken to either of them since."

"Has it always been that way?"

I shrugged. "She used to send me letters and all. Probably keeping it secret from my father. I don't know. But after I came out, that all dried up and died off. Haven't heard from her once since then."

"Shit. Colesy, I—"

"Cole," I cut in. "Just Cole."

"Cole," he repeated, his voice cracking on the word.

It felt good to hear my name falling from his lips that way. My teammates called me Colesy, and that was fine for them, but this thing with Luke...it felt different.

He brushed a thumb over my brow. An involuntary shiver coursed up my spine.

"I didn't have any idea it was so bad," Luke said. "Makes me feel like an ass for complaining about my family."

"You're not an ass."

"I have been. But I'm going to try not to be one anymore."

"Might be hard when you're around Dani," I pointed out wryly, but I couldn't stop myself from grinning. I knew she annoyed him, but deep down, they loved each other and they'd both bend over backwards for anyone in their family.

"True."

He scrunched up his nose, and I kissed him on the tip of it. Couldn't help myself. That nose was just begging to be kissed.

"But even when they're driving you crazy, it's because they love you."

"Yeah."

"They're pretty awesome that way." I kissed him again, this time on the lips—a long, soft, slow kiss that left me aching for more.

"You're pretty awesome yourself," he murmured, his lips still pressed to mine.

"And if we don't get a move on, we're going to be awesomely late for breakfast and maybe even the flight." I pinched him on the ass to get him up and moving. Besides, I liked touching his ass. I had about an hour to shower, dress, eat, pack, and get downstairs for the meeting. Immediately after that, we were flying to Minnesota for a game, and then we'd be flying home for another one against the Thunderbirds. "Come on. Gotta go."

Grudgingly, Luke crawled out from the comfort of the sheets and followed me into the bathroom. To save time, we jumped in the shower together. It took a hell of a lot of restraint to keep from shoving him up against the shower walls and having my way with him, since he was wet and slippery—and as hard as I was—but somehow, I refrained.

Once we were dry and dressed, he headed for the door so he could go back to his own room and pack up.

He'd just stepped out into the hall when I grabbed his hand and hauled him back for another kiss. I needed one more taste, and there was no telling when we'd be alone again. Probably not until tonight, at the soonest.

I tangled my hand in his hair, my tongue with his, pressing him against the frame of the door. It was a hard, hot, hungry kiss. Needy, even. I tried to put everything into the kiss that I wasn't ready to put into words, hoping he would understand.

"You'll make me late," he said, but it didn't sound like a complaint.

"We'll both be late."

But I couldn't make myself let him go. Not just yet. These times we had alone were too precious to me. I could breathe when I was with him, even when he got me to talk about my parents. I could be myself.

We were both sucking wind by the time I released him and sent him on his way to the hotel's elevator bay with a quick smack to his ass.

The look he tossed over his shoulder at me as he headed down the hall was pure heat.

I still wasn't sure what I'd started, and I was even less sure I was ready for the fallout. But even if I could turn back time and have a do-over, I doubted I would. I wanted this too much—not just to be with Luke but to *be myself*, and damn the consequences.

Maybe I'd intended to wait until I was retired to get involved with someone. But sometimes, life has other plans. And sometimes, those other plans are better than what you'd dreamed up to begin with. I had to count on this being one of those times.

The elevator doors opened. I watched until he stepped inside and the doors slid closed behind him. A sound at the other end of the hall caught my attention—something like the shutter to a camera—

but when I turned, there was no one there.

Must have been hearing things. This was an older hotel, after all—the architecture seemed to be mid-century or so. Old buildings tended to have strange sounds all the time.

Then I went back into my room and packed up all my clothes and personal items, preparing for the trip.

I could still feel the ghost of Luke's hands on me. Could still taste his lips and feel the slickness of his skin. Not even the revulsion of talking about my parents could eat away at the high I felt from being with him.

My belongings all packed, I headed down to join the rest of the team for breakfast before our flight, an undeniable bounce in my step.

Chapter Eleven

Cole

"Any of you boys hear anything new about Lennon?" Tony Bridger asked, setting down one of the cards from his hand and replacing it with another card from the draw pile.

Bridge was one of the new guys on the team this season, a fourth-line center who'd been spending a decent amount of time with me and Hammer on the penalty kill. The guy was something of a face-off specialist. He would've been an asset in helping Luke learn to take draws before preseason started, but Bridge hadn't been in town yet.

Then again, that ship had already sailed. Luke had a new focus now.

I stole a glance at the back of the plane, where Luke was in deep discussion with Anne and the rest of her crew, taking notes and occasionally piping up with a thought of his own. He would be working a camera at the game tonight—the first time she was trusting him with that sort of responsibility.

I couldn't help the warm rush of pride that flooded me every time I thought about how Luke was settling in at his new job. I'd played a small part in getting it for him, but that wasn't what made me proud—he was embracing this change of focus and seemed to be enjoying his new career. But I only allowed myself a moment before turning back to the card game.

The Lennon that Bridge was referring to would be Hayes Lennon, a top-line forward for the Thunderbirds, who'd been suspended due to allegedly beating up his girlfriend or something.

I supposed this was news we should all be aware of, though, since we'd be playing Tulsa in a couple of days. If Lennon wouldn't be on the ice, we should have a much easier time of beating the T-Birds—especially at home. With or without him, they were becoming a bigger threat than they had been even as little as a year ago, but it was never a bad thing to play a team without one of their best players.

I shook my head. "Haven't seen anything. What's new?"

Actually, I hadn't focused much on *any* of the news lately, whether about things going on in the hockey world or otherwise. I'd been too caught up in getting to know Luke Weber on a more intimate level to worry about some asshole who liked to hit women or the most recent debates politicians were raging over.

"Officially suspended pending results of the league's investigation," Hammer said. "And none too soon if you ask me." He drew a card, studied his hand,

and discarded a different one with a scowl.

"Sounds like there's not much evidence against him," Soupy said. "That's probably why the league dragged their feet."

"The team decided to suspend him before the league did," Bridge put in. He reached for a card and quirked up an eyebrow when he saw what it was.

"Because the Jernigans are terrified of scandal surrounding their church," Preston Hutchinson said, studying his hand and changing the order of a few of his cards. Hutch was relatively new to our team, too, having played in Tulsa during their first few seasons in the league. "Nothing more to it than that. Mrs. J probably shit a brick when she heard what he'd been accused of."

"You make it sound like you think he's innocent," I observed.

Hutch raised a brow and shook his head. "Lennon? The guy's a slimeball. Never liked him. I don't know if he did it or not. But my point is that Mrs. J just can't deal with anything like that. Whether he's guilty or not, she won't want him to be associated with the team— and with her church by association—for any longer than necessary. She's all about appearances. She cares more about what her congregation will think than she does about anything else."

"Sounds like a treat," I said. And I couldn't help but wonder how she would have reacted if I'd been playing for her team when I'd come out of the closet. Did she welcome homosexuals into her church family with open arms?

Something told me it wouldn't have gone well.

"At least there's one good thing about that," Hutch said.

"Yeah?" Soupy gave him a disbelieving look.

"It means we don't have to worry about Lennon being on the ice. They're a lot less dangerous without him up front."

True enough. And even though they weren't one of the better teams in the league, we'd all learned a long time ago that we should never count any team out. They could have a good night coinciding with us having a bad night, and the next thing we knew, they'd be beating us by a score of six to one or something. The Thunderbirds' top goaltender, Hunter Fielding, had been known to steal more than a few games.

I took another card from the draw pile. Still didn't have shit to work with in my hand. Picked a random card to discard because none of them were helping me anyway.

Before long, we were on the ground in Minnesota.

A brief stop at the hotel included a catered team meal. Anne and her crew were all with us for that, as well, but Luke stuck with them instead of joining me and the guys. Too bad. I doubted we would have done any flirtatious talking in front of the rest of the boys, but just having him near me would've been nice.

I was getting to be a little too attached to his presence. I liked having him around me so much that I physically missed him when he wasn't there. That was the only good explanation for the gnawing ache that filled my stomach.

But they were probably having a meeting over their meal, anyway. Anne worked crazy hours, and Luke was starting to follow in her footsteps where that was concerned.

After we ate, I looked over to where they'd been sitting, but he was already gone. It was just as well, since I needed to head up to my room for a nap before the game. We hadn't had a morning skate today, due to travel, so I at least needed to be well rested before puck drop tonight.

· · · · · ·

Hammer saucer-passed the puck over to me just before one of the Minny forwards slammed into him in an effort to knock the puck free. He grinned and shouted a few choice words at the guy, but I'd already skated the puck out of danger and was making my way up the ice with it. There were only two minutes left in the game, and we were tied. The boys and I all wanted to end it now. We needed two points in the standings, and more than that, we needed to keep the Wild from walking away with any.

Soupy was open, so I passed the puck to him. He could get it to his linemates. The guy wasn't as mobile as he used to be, but he could still pass as crisply and cleanly as anyone in the league. Probably because he'd spent hours a day for years passing the puck back and forth with his best friend, Eric Zellinger—our former captain, who was now playing in Tulsa.

Austin Cooper, one of our young forwards, had turned on his jets and was streaking in toward the Minnesota goal. Soupy managed to thread the needle, getting the puck between the two Minnesota defenders and right onto Coop's tape. But the Wild *D* were converging on him. He didn't have time to get a shot off.

They tied up his stick, and then it was a two-on-one fight to get the puck free. Somehow, he got his skate blade on it and kicked it back out to me.

I didn't stop to think. Didn't want to let my head get

in the way.

I pulled back my stick for a slap shot and slammed it home.

The Wild's goalie just got his glove on it, but he couldn't control the puck. It bounced away from him and headed straight for Hammer, of all people, who didn't waste any time. He just slapped the hell out of the puck, sending it back toward the Minnesota goal, since their goalie was still flailing to get back into position.

All three of our forwards converged on the goal.

The clock kept ticking down, with a mad crush of bodies all struggling for the puck just outside the blue paint of the goaltender's crease. I skated in and joined the melee in front of the net. Somehow, I got the toe of my skate on the puck.

It squirted free and headed straight for Coop's stick. He *just* got the blade of his stick on the puck in time to angle it into the net, right as the buzzer sounded.

The refs blew the whistle and convened at center ice to discuss what had happened.

"It went in," Coop shouted, skating after the zebras. "It fucking went in."

"You kicked it in," one of the Wild forwards countered. "Won't count."

"You fucking wish," he shot back.

But instead of waiting around to find out, Hammer casually skated over to the group of officials and listened in. Soupy followed him, keeping a bit of distance but still getting close enough to speak up if need be. Hammer said something to the refs, not that I could hear him, and then the two of them skated back to me.

"Going to have Toronto review it," Hammer said.

"But they're calling it a goal on the ice, so even if they can't determine it from video…"

It'd be a goal. That was the rule—the call on the ice stands if the video doesn't produce enough evidence to overturn it.

I nodded, skating back over to the bench to fill in the coaching staff and the rest of my teammates.

A minute later, one of the referees put on the mic for the arena's loudspeaker system and announced that the play was under review. His mic cut out halfway through his pronouncement, but everyone caught the drift.

The crowd was restless. You could almost hear a fucking pin drop in the place. For an arena that could be unbelievably loud at times, the silence was disconcerting.

Usually, the in-arena entertainment team would start playing music during a video review, but it appeared they were having difficulties. Even the Jumbotron over the center of the ice was malfunctioning. It was just showing black-and-white static. The silence only made the crowd more restless.

And then it happened. Someone high up in the stands shouted, "Fucking faggot!" It echoed through the arena, the one thing that could be made out among the general crowd noise.

I couldn't tell where, exactly, it'd come from. Didn't care. All I knew was I wanted to crawl into a hole and not come out again for a very long time.

Then it wasn't quiet in the arena any longer. More people started shouting, even louder than the first guy.

"Queer!"

"Fucking homo!"

"We don't want you here."

But there were other shouts, too. "Get out of here. Take your hate and go home."

"Mind your own damned business!"

"He's not hurting anyone."

Then there were so many people shouting, nothing anyone said could be made out. It was just a big mess of anger and hatred.

A shouting match that no one could win.

I didn't even think anyone was trying to win. They just wanted to shout for the sake of shouting, not to be heard.

The tension was so thick it felt as if the whole arena was about to explode.

This was *exactly* why I'd wanted to keep my secret until I wasn't playing any longer.

"Ignore it," Hammer said in my ear.

I nodded, but I couldn't ignore it. My head was swimming. I felt nauseated.

And Luke was here somewhere, too. Filming it? Probably. I had to wonder if Anne or any of the other guys on her team were with him… If he was alone in the midst of this somewhere…

If he was okay.

I scanned the crowd, but I'd never be able to find him out there. Trying was futile.

Our head coach, Mattias Bergstrom, caught my eye, and he waved me over to the end of the bench. "You want to come off?" he asked.

I glared at him in return. "I'm not running and hiding from this."

He nodded. "Didn't think you would. But I thought I'd offer."

"I'm good," I bit off. Swallowing hard, I nodded my thanks and skated back over to the rest of my teammates on the ice. I caught Webs's eye as I went. He looked as pissed as I felt.

And scared, just like me.

Probably thinking about Luke, too. Probably worried about his kid.

I wished there were something I could say, something that would make it easier for him, but there wasn't anything. What could anyone say to ease the sting of ignorant hatred?

Finally, the ref who'd been on the phone in the scorekeeper's box skated back over to join the others. He spoke to them for a minute, then to each of the coaches. When he tried to turn on his mic, the sound system still refused to work.

But the crowd could easily make out that he was signaling a goal. We'd won the game, and the crowd erupted into an even bigger fit than before. Some of the fans tossed things onto the ice—beers, hats, popcorn containers, and all sorts of other game-going paraphernalia—and the coaching staffs and building security hustled both teams down the tunnel toward the dressing rooms.

We'd won the game, but it felt like shit.

And I still didn't know if Luke was somewhere safe.

Nausea threatened to overwhelm me, and I had to take a moment in the concourse to gather myself together. I pressed my forehead against the cool wall, struggling to breathe.

Koz, of all people, stopped and waited for me. He passed a bottle of water into my hands.

I dumped the whole thing over my head. I desperately needed to cool off, much more than I needed to drink it. And besides, if I'd tried to swallow it right now, I might have upchucked everything inside me.

He slapped me on the back a couple of times. "Come on. He'll be okay. Same as you will. People suck, but he'll be okay."

I couldn't form the words to ask him what he was talking about.

"Let's get back to the room. That's where they'll bring him."

Somehow, I managed to force my legs to move, my feet to take one step and then another, until we were at the door to the locker room.

I didn't fall apart.

But there were only frayed threads holding me together.

Chapter Twelve

Luke

I knew I had a job to do. I knew Anne and the rest of the guys were counting on me. But at a time like this, I couldn't do it. I *couldn't*. I just plain didn't have it in me.

Because the son of a bitch who'd started the chant had been staring straight at me while he shouted his hatred and obscenities.

Careful to protect the camera equipment Anne had entrusted me with, I backed away from the alcohol-fueled asshole and headed for the concourse.

A building security guard stopped me when I'd barely made it ten steps. "Come with me."

"I didn't do anything wrong," I spluttered, immediately thinking he was going to try to arrest me or something. Apparently, my mind automatically jumped to the worst thing that could be happening at a time like this. I fumbled for my badge that was hanging around my neck. "I'm authorized to film—"

"I'm trying to get you back to the visiting team's locker rooms faster, sir. Come on. Let's go before this blows up any worse than it already has."

Oh. Yeah, that was probably a good idea. I followed him to an elevator bank, and he swiped a badge of his own to get it to open.

"Nobody hurt you?" he asked.

I shook my head, but that made me realize that every other part of me was shaking, too. "Not physically," I managed to get out.

"Some people can be real pricks," he said quietly after an awkward moment of eerie silence, following the cacophony in the stands.

The elevator came to a stop, and once the doors opened, I followed him through the concrete tunnels until we reached the visiting team's area.

Anne was the first person I saw. She rushed over and flung her arms around my neck, nearly strangling me with the intensity of her hug. "Don't let it get to you," she said. "Try to forget it ever happened. They're just ignorant assholes."

But however much I might like to, I couldn't just brush it off and pretend it hadn't happened.

That guy had been yelling *at me*. And at Cole, too, I supposed. But honestly, he'd been looking straight at me when he'd started.

Still, I nodded. "I'm fine," I said.

"No, you're not, but you will be." She took the equipment from my shaking hands, handed it off to Dave, and led me to a bench, pushing on my shoulders until I took a seat.

A minute later, the team started to come in from the ice. I couldn't help it that my eyes searched the sea of faces until they landed on Cole. He looked as freaked out as I felt.

Even though everything in me was screaming to run to him and wrap him up in my arms, I stayed put.

We were on his turf now. It was his move. His call to make if he wanted to do something like that when his teammates were around.

Dad and the rest of the coaches filed into the room once all the players were in their stalls and stripping out of their gear. The security guard who'd brought me in headed over and said a few words to them, which made me even more uncomfortable than I already was. Especially when I felt Dad's eyes move over to me. I didn't want to look at him, but I couldn't seem to stop it from happening. He was listening to the security guy, but his focus was entirely on me.

He looked pissed. Scared and pissed.

I hated that I'd been the cause of it. If I hadn't been here, he could just be concerned about his players. He wouldn't have to be worried about me, too.

I felt sure he was going to come over and do a Dad Thing, like pull me in for a hug or something, and then I'd end up breaking down. That was *not* what I wanted to happen right now. I didn't want to fall apart. I just wanted to get myself together enough that I could stop shaking, and then we could get the hell out of here. And once I was alone somewhere, *then* I could fall apart.

But he surprised me by walking over to Cole, instead.

I dropped my gaze to my feet because I didn't want to lose it. A lifetime ticked by. Or maybe it was only a minute or two.

And then Cole reached for my hand.

We were in the middle of the locker room. Surrounded by his teammates, including assholes like Koz. What the hell was he doing?

But he laced his fingers through mine, and he tugged me up, and then we were walking out into the hallway together, hand in hand.

I felt my father's gaze following us. His and everyone else's.

My heart seemed to have lodged in my throat. My lungs wouldn't fill properly. I knew I'd break down if I tried to speak, so I bit my tongue and held it all inside.

Cole stopped once we were alone and couldn't be overheard. He backed me up against the wall and tipped my chin, forcing me to meet his gaze.

"Are you okay?" he asked, searching my eyes.

I nodded, swallowing hard.

"They told your father that the guys who started it were yelling at you."

"Near me," I croaked. And then I wondered why Dad had told Cole instead of coming to me himself. Usually, he would try to handle these things on his own. But this time, he'd handed the job off to someone else.

"*At* you," Cole corrected.

I forced my head to jerk into a terse nod. For some reason, it hurt more to acknowledge the truth than it did to skirt it.

He studied me so hard I thought I might melt under his scrutiny. "No one tried to hurt you?"

"Not physically." But we both knew that physical pain would be much easier to bear. This kind of pain cut all the way to the core of a person. It left scars that would never heal. I knew he had more than his fair share of them, too.

Sometimes, living in this world really sucked.

But other times, there couldn't be anything better. Somehow, now was one of *those* moments, because Cole was with me, and I was with him, and the shit going on in the world didn't seem to matter as much when he looked at me this way—like he could see all the way into my soul, like he knew all the things rushing through my head without me having to say them aloud.

When he touched me like this—like he wanted to protect me from all the shit in the world that no one could protect anyone from.

There wasn't anything sexual to the way he was holding me. It was all about comfort—about reassuring both of us that we were okay. His strong arms wrapped tightly around me, and I melted into the warmth of his touch.

We both needed it. We needed each other.

"This is my fault," he ground out, his voice harsh and rough next to my ear.

"Your fault? How do you figure that?"

Reluctantly, he released me enough to be able to look into my eyes. "When I kissed you in the hall of the hotel…there was a photographer hidden somewhere."

I still didn't follow, and my confusion must have shown all over my face.

"The pictures hit social media just before the game, apparently, and it blew up. We're trending on Twitter in the U.S. and Canada. They've even given us a hashtag… #hockeyisgay. It's the biggest story being talked about on Facebook, even bigger than all the political crap in Washington right now. Instagram, too.

We've gone viral."

"Shit. I'm so sorry," I said. Maybe I'd wanted to be a trailblazer for gay athletes, or at least for gay hockey players, but Cole and I both knew he'd never wanted anything of the sort. This had to be an absolute nightmare for him. He just wanted to go about his business, do his job and live his life without anyone interfering in it.

"You're sorry?" His brow hitched up almost comically. "I'm the one who mauled you in the hall. This is on me. But now we're both having to deal with the aftermath."

I knew I shouldn't laugh at a time like this, but I couldn't help it. My laughter bubbled up and boiled over, and I couldn't rein it in to save my life.

"What's so funny?"

I shrugged, trying to bite down on my cheek to make the laughter stop. No use, though. "Just that if anyone's around with a camera right now, you might as well be mauling me in the hall again. And maybe it's not funny, but I bet your parents are going to flip out over this. It's like their worst nightmare or something."

His lips quirked up into the hot-as-fuck smile I loved so much. "So should we give them a show? I don't think there are any rogue cameras down here, but I bet we could get Anne to help us out…"

In lieu of answering, I grabbed hold of the back of his skull and tugged him down for a scorching kiss.

Maybe some people didn't like the idea of two dudes kissing. Maybe it scared them or made them question their own sexuality. Who the hell knew what made them hateful sons of bitches? I sure didn't.

All I knew was that kissing Cole Paxton was the best thing happening in my life right now, and I didn't want anything to put a damper on that.

The sound of a man clearing his throat a few feet away got Cole to break off the kiss—gradually—so we could both see who was interrupting us.

Dad had his arms crossed, his legs braced apart in a familiar, intimidating stance.

"You need something?" I asked. Because I knew all the shit he'd put Jamie and Cody through, and I didn't want to deal with him putting Cole through the same things.

"Just needed to see for myself that you're okay. But it looks like Colesy's got things under control."

We both burst out laughing, all the tension and ugliness of the last thirty minutes or so starting to flow away with the hilarity.

Dad narrowed his eyes. "Don't be an asswipe, Colesy."

"All right." Cole sobered up almost instantly. "Would asking Luke to move in with me get me out of asswipe territory? Or move me deeper into it? Because if we're already dealing with shit like this, I guess we might as well make it official."

Sparklers might as well have just lit up in my stomach. It was like a mini-explosion going on inside me.

"I don't know," Dad said slowly, and I felt the heat of his stare shifting over to settle on me. "Depends on Luke's take on the situation."

"Luke thinks it's good," I said, my voice floundering. I cleared my throat and tried again. "I think it's really good." I met my father's gaze head on and made sure he understood my meaning, and then I reached for Cole's hand.

His fingers curled possessively around mine.

"You serious?" I asked.

"As a heart attack."

"What about your parents? This is all blowing up… It's only going to get worse."

"My parents wrote me off a long time ago. I don't care what they think. They probably don't care what I do, anyway. Except when they think it'll affect them in some way."

My dad had been quiet during the last few exchanges, but now he stepped forward, his face full of emotion. I blinked in surprise, hoping he wasn't about to burst into tears on me or something. But instead, Dad wrapped Cole up in a massive bear hug, lifting him off his feet in his exuberance.

It wasn't the kind of hug hockey players usually give one another—the sort with lots of back-slapping, pushing-and-shoving machismo. It was a Dad Hug, the kind he usually gave to me and my sisters—not anything I'd expect him to give one of his players.

Cole blinked in shock when Dad set him back down on his feet. "What was that for?" he spluttered.

Just like that, Dad's regular gruff manner was back. He crossed his arms over his chest again. "A guy needs a hug from a dad every now and then. Doesn't necessarily have to be his own dad giving it," he said. Then he spun on his heel to head back the other way. "But you'd still better not be an asswipe, Colesy," he called over his shoulder.

Chapter Thirteen

Cole

After the Thunderbirds game, all anyone seemingly wanted to talk about was Leif "Thor" Sorenson's slapper to the balls of Thunderbirds' defenseman Ethan Higgins. I felt sorry for Higgins, but I had to admit to being glad the hockey world had shifted the focus away from me, Luke, and the homophobic incident in Minnesota.

Higgins had hit the ice like a tree falling in the forest, only no one had bothered to shout "Timber!" He was practically as big as a tree, too. As if a slap shot to the balls wasn't bad enough, hitting the ice from that high when he probably wasn't bracing himself for the fall…

Ouch. Seriously…ouch.

Just thinking about taking a ninety-plus-mile-an-hour slap shot to the balls was enough to make my eyes water, so I'd been shocked to see him back on the ice later in the game. It served to prove the old adage that hockey players were tough as nails, though. I hoped for his sake that they'd at least given him some sort of numbing shot to help him get through the rest of the night. An ice pack would help, but I doubted it'd be enough for me if I were in his shoes.

Besides, I wasn't sure I could stand to hold an ice pack on my balls for long enough for the numbing effects to help. Ice and certain body parts didn't seem to be a good combination.

Koz had organized a bunch of the guys to go out after the game. He'd invited some of our former teammates who were now playing for the Thunderbirds to come along, as well. But I wasn't in the mood.

I'd much prefer to spend some time with Luke.

Instead of letting Koz drag me into something I didn't want to be part of, I shot off a text message to Luke once I'd showered and finished up all my post-game responsibilities, asking what he wanted to do. There was a part of me—not a small one, either—that hoped he'd suggest coming over to my place and spending the night.

I was prepared for him to shoot me down, for any number of potential reasons. Things had to be different between us when we were in Portland than they'd been on the road. And the fallout from our social media scandal and the incident in Minnesota was bound to still be affecting him. It'd probably be fucking with both of us for a long time to come. Shit like that could change a person, and not always for the better.

I *hoped* it was serving to draw us closer together—helping us to see what was truly important and block out the rest—but that remained to be seen. Neither of us had really had enough time to process it yet.

I wasn't quite prepared for the response I got, though.

Luke: *Mom wants you to come over.*

Wait, what? Why did Laura Weber want me to come to her house? She'd never been one to demand my presence anywhere or for anything. Even when they'd had that barbecue in the backyard, I'd been invited, not ordered to appear.

I couldn't wrap my head around it. But still, I sent him a quick reply.

Me: *When? This weekend or something?*

Luke: *Nope. Now.*

Me: *Tonight?*

Luke: *Yep. Tonight. Now.*

Me: *For real? You're not shitting me, are you?*

Luke: *She's serious. And when Mom decides something, we have to do it whether we want to or not. That's the way it works in my family.*

Me: *If that's what you want, okay.*

Luke: *Not sure if I want it, and I'm even less sure you should. But one thing about my mom*

*is she always gets her way. You might as well
just learn that now if we're going to be together.
So I guess we're going.*

Me: *I guess we are. Meet you at my car in 15?*

Luke: *Done.*

I finished cleaning up and changing clothes as quickly as I could, and then I headed for the parking garage. Luke was waiting there for me. I stole a quick peck before we climbed in, even though I wanted a hell of a lot more.

"You seriously don't have any idea what this is about?" I asked, pulling out of my parking spot.

"If I knew, I would've told you. Mom's kind of cryptic about things sometimes. She'll tell us in her own good time."

We didn't talk much on the drive, but it was a comfortable sort of silence. My radio was blaring some classic pop tunes from the eighties, some of which Luke knew all the words to even though they were from before he was born. Maybe we should've stuck around for karaoke that night before the season started, after all. I made a mental note to take him back to a karaoke bar sometime—without his sisters and my teammates. It could be fun if it was just the two of us.

By the time I pulled into his parents' driveway and shut off the engine, we were both feeling relaxed and ready to face whatever Laura might throw at us.

Luke let himself in the front door without bothering to knock. That's not something I would have ever done at my parents' house now that I was an adult. I was an outsider as far as they were concerned—not family.

Certainly not someone who could feel free to come and go as he pleased. But then again, Luke did live here, at least for now, so I supposed it wasn't such a surprise.

When we walked into the living room, Laura was on the couch with her shoes off and her feet up, one arm draped across the back of the cushions. A bottle of red wine waited on the coffee table alongside two wineglasses.

"Hey, baby," she said, grinning when she saw her son. "Your sisters are in the kitchen. I need you to go help them."

"Help them with what?" Luke asked warily. He shot a glance in my direction, as if to ask what was going on.

But this was his family, not mine. He probably had a much better idea than I could ever come up with. I shrugged.

"Just go," Laura said. "I need a word with Cole, and that means I need you to clear out."

I raised my brows at him in question.

He shook his head. "Dad's a lot scarier than she is, though. You'll be fine. She's probably just planning to ply you with wine and grill you about your intentions or something."

Laura scowled at her son. "I'm not plying anyone with wine."

"Mm hmm," he murmured, but he was already heading for the kitchen. "That's why you've got two glasses there, right? Because you've started drinking out of two glasses at the same time?"

She playfully tossed a pillow at his retreating form. Once he was gone, she turned serious eyes on me. "Have a seat, Cole. You and I need to have a talk, and I don't want us to be interrupted."

No matter how shitty my parents had been, I'd been

raised to have good manners. When a lady told me to do something, I did as I was told.

So I sat. But at this point, I was far more wary than curious.

She uncorked the wine bottle and poured two glasses, wordlessly offering one to me by holding it aloft with a questioning look. Luke might have been right, whether she wanted to admit it or not.

Still, I accepted the glass when she offered it to me. "Thanks," I said, taking a cautious sip. Not that I expected poison—I just didn't know what she wanted, and I had no intention of getting so drunk that I gave her anything I didn't plan to.

But she didn't keep me in suspense for long. "David told me that you've asked Luke to move in with you."

I almost choked on my wine, which would've been a damn shame, because it was a really nice Shiraz. I did appreciate her getting straight to the point, though.

"I did," I replied once I'd managed to swallow the wine without incident.

"Do you intend to marry him?"

"I'm not— We haven't talked about that yet. And to be honest, I think it'd be better for me to talk about these things with Luke before I talk to anyone else. He deserves that much."

She took another sip from her wineglass, eyeing me shrewdly over the rim. "Fair enough. What about kids?"

This time, even though I wasn't prepared for the impertinence of her question, I kept the fluids from going down the wrong pipe. I set the glass down on the coffee table, shaking my head. "Do you really think I'd answer that when, again, I haven't talked to your son about it yet? Besides, we're not at that point yet.

We're talking about living together. That's all." So far...

"Do you want them?" she demanded. "Gay couples can adopt these days. It's happening all the time."

"I'm aware of that."

"Is that something you'd want? A family? With Luke?"

I wanted a family, yeah. Kids weren't something I'd ever allowed myself to think about, because I'd planned to avoid relationships entirely until I was out of the public eye. But I had to admit, I liked the idea of starting with parents who cared—like the Webers clearly did—and maybe some siblings like Katie and Dani, even if Dani tended to shove her nose into places she had no business shoving it.

My chest ached with wanting those things. I wanted to belong. I wanted to have people who cared as much for me as I did for them. As much as Luke's family clearly cared for him. I wanted a mother who meddled and a father who blustered and threatened, and I even wanted sisters who got on my last fucking nerve. I wanted an extended family who would come over for a backyard barbecue on the spur of a moment and accept whatever decision I made for myself, my future, my family.

I wanted a *family*. A real family full of people who cared more about me and what was going on in my life than they did for appearances and how that would affect their corporate dollars.

I wanted what Luke had so much it hurt. And I wanted even more of it—*with him*.

But for whatever reason, I couldn't seem to put that into words. They stuck in my throat, strangling me and making my eyes burn.

Without hesitation, Laura set down her wine and crossed over to me, wrapping me up in her arms. "Okay. It's okay. You don't have to have an answer right now. But just know that if you two decide it is something you want, you'll have our complete support. We'll do whatever it takes to make sure of it. Because we love you and we want you to be happy."

Luke and Dani came back into the living room then, with me close to becoming a puddle in their mother's arms. They stopped short, and I quickly separated myself from Laura and tried to get my shit together.

"What the hell, Mom?" Luke demanded.

"She's fine," I said before he could go off on her. This wasn't a reason for him to be mad at his mother. It was one of the best things I'd ever experienced. "It's fine."

He scowled.

"Promise," I said. "It's really okay."

Eventually, he let it go—at least for now—and we all sat around drinking Laura's wine and talking. Well, all but Dani. She looked grumpy as she sipped on flavored water while we played Cards Against Humanity together. Babs, Harry, and Webs eventually joined us—and then the game turned *really* inappropriate.

Admittedly, it felt a bit awkward to play a game like that with Luke's parents. At least it did at first. But before long, I started to let go of my inhibitions and recognize the experience for what it was.

For the first time, I was truly being accepted as part of this family.

There wasn't anywhere I'd rather be.

L ate that night, lying in bed together after we'd shared mutual blow jobs, I rested my chin on Cole's chest and stared up into his eyes. He'd started to let his facial hair grow like he sometimes did during the season.

I liked the scruff. I liked it a hell of a lot.

For that matter, I liked just about everything about this man. Yeah, I'd had a massive crush on him for a long time, but getting to know the *real* Cole was so much better than my idealized version of him. He wasn't just a hot hockey player with a job I wished I could have. He had scruff I liked feeling against my balls. He was kind and thoughtful. He helped me to see the good I had going on in my life.

Hell, *he* was responsible for so much of that good.

But there was a deep thought creasing his brow as he stared back down at me, the blue of his eyes almost black in concentration.

"You look awfully serious for a guy who just got off," he said, brushing my hair off my forehead.

I could've said the same to him. Still, serious? Yeah, I supposed I was feeling serious. It was hard not to be lost in thought after what I'd walked in on earlier at my parents' house.

"What'd Mom want with you tonight?" I asked.

"Same as your dad."

"She wanted to tell you not to be an asswipe?" I couldn't keep the drollness from invading my tone.

He laughed. "Not exactly."

"Then what, exactly?"

"I guess you could say she wanted to know my intentions as far as you're concerned."

"You're not serious."

"Pretty serious," he replied.

"She wants to know when you're gonna put a ring on it? Sorry. She can be a bit pushy about that kind of shit. I don't expect—"

"Not in so many words, no," he cut in. "And she wasn't exactly pushing me. She'll let us figure this out on our own."

I scoffed.

He chuckled. "She will. But it was…different than with your dad, I guess you could say."

"Different how?" I kept absentmindedly stroking the smattering of hair on his chest.

He captured my fingers in his and forced me to stop. I focused on his eyes. They'd gone dark with intensity, and he didn't blink, didn't do anything to hide from my scrutiny.

"Different in that she wanted me to know that I can have a family now if I want it. With you," he added.

"She wants grandchildren. She'll do anything for grandkids."

"It wasn't about kids or whatever. She didn't get into that much. It was more about the rest of it."

"You mean she said you can have an interfering mother, an overprotective father, and a couple of sisters who get on your last fucking nerve at least once every few hours?"

"Not in so many words." But his grin confirmed it.

"They'll all annoy the shit out of you soon."

"I can't fucking wait."

"I'll remind you of that when you're ready to strangle Mom because she won't keep her nose out of our business and wishing something would cause permanent damage to Dani's vocal chords."

"And I'll remind *you* how awesome they are when we take our kids to backyard family barbecues at your parents' house to play with their cousins and we all drink wine and play Cards Against Humanity in the kitchen after the kids have passed out together in the blanket fort your dad builds for them in the living room."

"Our kids?" I asked. I kind of liked the sound of that. Cole would be a good dad. The way he'd been looking after me for the last couple of months proved it.

"We don't have to decide anything about that yet," he hurried to say. "But I just started thinking about it while I was talking with your mom. I mean, we haven't even talked about us being an *us* yet, let alone—"

"I want *us* to be a thing," I cut in.

"Yeah?" His grin was sexy as hell.

"Yeah. I mean, we don't have to put a ring on it yet, but—"

"But we're together," he said. "You and me. We're going to do this."

"Might as well, since the whole world already saw us making out in the hall of a hotel."

He caught my lower lip between his teeth and kissed me hard, his tongue making a quick swipe into my mouth to tangle with mine. In no time, we were both panting for air and hard again. He fisted his hands in my hair and let out a fierce, possessive sound when he broke off the kiss.

"I want you to move in with me," he said. "I want to come home to you every night."

"Yeah?"

"Yeah. And I even want your mom sticking her nose in our business all the time, and your dad threatening me about being an asswipe when I screw things up with you. And I want your sisters annoying us all the time. I want it all."

"Good. Maybe I'll let *you* deal with them so I don't have to."

"You'll still have to," he said, but he rolled over so he was on top of me, pinning me to the bed. "We'll deal with them together. I want a *family*, Luke. I want your family to be my family. Even when they annoy the shit out of both of us. Hell, especially then—because it means they care."

"I'll leave you to deal with them," I said. But I was laughing so hard because this was the best way to spend an evening ever.

"Deal. Whatever you want. Because I want *you* to be my family."

"I like the sound of that," I said. I liked it more than I could say.

"I think I love you, Luke."

"You'd better. Because I've been in love with you since before I knew it would be okay. Maybe in lust, not in love—at first. But still."

"You had a crush on me?" he asked, and his grin was kind of cocky, but it was a hot sort of cocky, not a turn-off sort of cocky. I doubted there was anything Cole Paxton could do that would ever be a turn-off for me. Everything he did only seemed to rev me up more than I already was.

"That was kind of how I realized I was gay," I admitted. "Couldn't stop thinking about you."

"I'm going to file that one away for later."

"For later?"

"Yep. For when I need ammunition to convince you to marry me or something."

We were both laughing when I kissed him again.

I could get used to this. I could absolutely get used to this.

And there wasn't a single reason why I shouldn't.

Epilogue

Cole

These days, if Anne didn't have Luke working through lunch, he tended to come out to Amani's with me and the rest of the guys on game days.

None of the boys seemed to mind having him around, and I knew it helped him to feel as if he were still part of a team. Yeah, he was settling into his new job nicely, and he was really enjoying it. But there's something about being surrounded by a group of hockey players, especially when it's what you've been doing your whole life, like he had. It was helping to ease his transition into his post-hockey life.

Not gonna lie—I liked having him with me. It was as good for me as it was for him, because I'd meant every bit of what I'd told him. He was my family now, and frankly, I'd been starved for family affection. He kept saying I'd get sick of his parents and his sisters and the way they were constantly interfering with us, but I doubted it. He didn't really hate it, anyway. It was just second nature for him to gripe about them. He'd miss it like crazy if they suddenly stopped.

And I was proud as fuck of the way he was adjusting to his new normal, too.

It couldn't be easy for him. Hell, I was worried about how I'd handle the transition to being a former pro hockey player, even though I still had (hopefully) a few years left before I made that change. But Luke had already become fully engaged in his new job, and he was even making himself invaluable to Anne.

With every on-ice situation that came up, he was in her ear, talking her through what was happening so she wouldn't have to dig through a rule book to understand it.

When she'd needed an idea for a segment last week, he'd been quick to come up with something—he took the viewers into the trainers' room after a practice so everyone could see how hard it is for the older guys to stay in game shape every day.

It might not be exciting to watch a bunch of hockey players in their late thirties being stretched and put into ice baths and all, but he made it into good viewing because he managed to bring out our personalities and the way we teased each other about who was the oldest and most broken. News flash: Soupy was *definitely* the player most likely to fall apart the next time a strong breeze blew his way. He was held together by gorilla glue and duct tape these days.

Koz was down at the other end of the table, at least, with Babs on one side of him and Jonny on the other. Not only that, but the guy had his nose buried in his phone. Probably for the best. If he was caught up in that, he couldn't put his foot in his mouth and say something Koz-like that would make me want to rip out his throat.

The waiter brought out a bunch of dishes and spread them out across the center of the table—pastas, fresh salads, grilled chicken, seafood, beef, and almost everything else imaginable for a homestyle Italian place. Finally, Koz set down his phone, but it was only so he could stuff his face.

It didn't matter how many times I'd eaten here over the years. My mouth still watered every time a pan of fresh lasagna landed right in front of me. The cheese was ooey-gooey melting over the top and crispy around the edges of the pan. Luke and I both reached for it at the same time, our hands bumping over the serving spoon.

He gave me a sheepish look.

I put a big portion on his plate before doing the same with my own. Not a problem for me that my man had excellent taste. It was one more way I could be sure we'd get along well for a long time to come. Compatibility in the kitchen was just as important in a relationship as compatibility in the bedroom.

I was just about to dig in when my phone buzzed in my pocket.

Not just my phone, either. Almost every guy sitting around the table reached for his phone.

Huh. Weird.

Luke gave me a questioning look as I took it out and swiped the screen to see what was going on.

It was a text message from Jim Sutter.

If any of you are with Blake Kozlow, tell him

*to delete the Tweet NOW and to get over to
my office ASAP so we can do damage control.*

Babs ripped Koz's phone from his hands before any
of the rest of us could react.

"The fuck are you doing?" Koz demanded.

But Babs had moved away from the table, and
Jonny put a hand on Koz's shoulder, keeping him in
his seat.

I opened my Twitter app and went to Koz's profile
to see what the hell he'd done. Some random fan had
tagged him in a Tweet about the Lennon incident in
Tulsa, and instead of ignoring it, he'd done the
unthinkable: Koz had replied, "Must be a retard to
think it's okay to hit chicks."

"Seriously, dude?" Babs said when he finally looked
up from Koz's phone. "Do you never fucking think?"

Koz tried to shrug free from Jonny's grip, but there
wasn't much point in trying. "I don't—"

"You can't use words like that," 501 bit out, looking
ready to deck the guy. Not that I could blame him.

"I wasn't— I just—" The words came out in a
splutter. "Christ, I didn't fucking mean anything by it.
Hell, if anyone's a retard around here, it's me."

"Don't we all know it," Luke muttered beneath his
breath, and I had to bite down on the inside of my
cheek to stop myself from bursting into inappropriate
laughter. Now wasn't the time.

This was sure to be a PR nightmare for the team,
and not one I had any intention of being involved in.
I'd had my fill of those lately, and I might have to deal
with even more than my fair share of them if and when
Luke and I ever *did* decide to get married. Or adopt
kids. Or do anything else that brought us back into the

spotlight.

I caught his eye and grabbed my plate, angling my head toward a quieter table away from the rest of the team. "Wanna head over there?"

Relief flooded his face as he grabbed his plate and followed me. The rest of the guys were still caught up in giving Koz shit for being a dumb ass, so no one bothered to rag on us for slipping away.

My phone pinged again. In case it was something to do with the Koz situation, I checked it—because none of the other guys were likely to hear their phones over the shouting match that was going on.

It wasn't from Jim Sutter or any of the coaches, though. In fact, it wasn't from anyone to do with the team at all.

It was from my mother. I still had her cell phone number programmed in mine, not that I'd bothered to use it in ages.

My mouth went dry.

"What's wrong?" Luke demanded.

"Wrong?" I repeated, feeling numb.

"You're white as a sheet."

But I couldn't answer him. Not until I knew what she wanted.

Bracing myself against hurt because I refused to give either of my parents that kind of control over me, I swiped my thumb across the screen to read the message.

It was a *long* message, too.

> *I just thought you should know that your father is facing his biggest scandal yet with his company. Not only is his gay son flaunting his gayness by having a gay relationship that's out*

in the open, but his wife is filing for divorce.

I left him last week. Nothing has been made public yet, but it will be as soon as the court documents are filed.

I know I wasn't always there for you. I know you needed me to be. I know I haven't been a good mother for you. I know I should have tried harder and that I failed because I didn't.

But I'm tired of living under his thumb, and I hope we can find a way to make amends. I'd really like to meet Luke sometime. Only if you're okay with that, of course. If you're not, I'll understand. It will hurt, but I'll understand.

I'm sure there've been a lot of ways I've hurt you, maybe even ways I don't realize, so I don't expect you to forgive me overnight. I'm sure you may never be able to forgive me, and if that's the case, I'll just have to come to terms with that. But I had to try. I wish I'd tried sooner, but I am trying now.

Please consider allowing me to meet your boyfriend. I can come to you. We can do this on your terms, or not at all, if that's what you decide.

I'm sorry, Cole. And please know that I love you. I've always loved you, even if I haven't always done a very good job of showing that.

I had to blink back tears after reading it.

"What?" Luke reached across the table and took my hand—a surprisingly public gesture, but one that I needed. It helped me to pull myself together again.

"My mother wants to meet you," I forced myself to say, somehow managing to avoid breaking down in the middle of the restaurant.

"Yeah?" He cocked up a brow. "Is that a good thing or a bad thing?"

"I think it's a good thing." I hoped it was, at least.

"So are we going to do this?"

"I think so."

"But not your father," he said, matter-of-factly.

"No, not my father."

"Okay." And just like that, he'd accepted the news that had hit me over the head like a hammer.

"Okay?"

"Yeah, okay. If you want me to meet her, I'll meet her. I can't promise I won't give her an earful about how shitty she's been to you, though."

I couldn't stop the laugh from bubbling up inside me. "Pretty sure she's fully aware of that, based on what she had to say.

He cocked up a brow in question, so I shoved my phone over so he could read it all. "Still not making any promises," he said around a mouthful of lasagna after reading through the message in its entirety. "Maybe she's just saying what she thinks you want to hear. Maybe she doesn't really mean all of it."

I shrugged. "Maybe not. But I think it's worth finding out. Don't you?"

He took another bite, chewed thoughtfully, and swallowed. "Yeah, I do. Because family's important."

He had that one right. Family was more important than a lot of people would ever understand. Until you didn't have one, sometimes you took them for granted.

Luke turned his head on a swivel for a moment, but I had no clue what he was looking for. Then he wiped his mouth on his napkin and set the cloth on the table, standing up.

I gave him a questioning look, but he shook his head and went back to the main table. Koz and a few of the other guys had gone—no doubt Jonny and a couple of others had hauled him out of the restaurant and back up to the team's practice facility so he could deal with the fallout of his poor decision-making. When Luke returned, it was with the lasagna pan in his hands.

"Excellent thinking," I said.

"Priorities, right?"

Right. Good lasagna was definitely a priority. But not as much of one as being myself, no matter who was watching. And not as much as holding on to family. With Luke in my life, I had a feeling it would be a hell of a lot easier to keep my priorities straight.

Roster

Name	Position	Nickname	Number
Cole Paxton	Defense	Colesy	3
Lauri Vanhanen	Defense	Van	4*
Levi Babcock	Defense*	501	5
Chris Hammond	Defense	Hammer	6
Keith Burns	Defense	Burnzie	7
Cody Williams	Defense	Harry	8
Brenden Campbell	Left Wing	Soupy	11
Andrei Sokolov	Center	Socks	13
Blake Kozlow	Center	Koz	14
Austin Cooper	Center	Coop	16
Jamie Babcock	Right Wing	Babs	19
Axel Johansson	Right Wing	Jo-Jo	20
Dylan Poplawski	Right Wing	Pops	21
Leif Sorenson	Defense	Thor	24
Cam Johnson	Left Wing	Jonny	28
Nicklas Ericsson	Goal	Nicky	30
Konrad Jokelainen	Goal	Loki	32
Preston Hutchinson	Left Wing	Hutch	39
Aaron Ludwiczak	Left Wing	Luddy	43
Tony Bridger	Center	Bridge	62
Nate Golston	Left Wing	Ghost	83
Riley Jezek	Center	RJ	91

About the Author

Catherine Gayle is a USA Today bestselling author of Regency-set historical romance and contemporary hockey romance. She's a transplanted Texan living in North Carolina with two extremely spoiled felines. In her spare time, she watches way too much hockey and reality TV, plans fun things to do for the Nephew Monster's next visit, and performs experiments in the kitchen which are rarely toxic.

Visit her website at www.catherinegayle.com. Join her mailing list at http://eepurl.com/GXcwr to receive news about new releases, sales, and pre-orders, as well as to receive a free Portland Storm short story titled ICE BREAKER, which is not available for sale through

Other Books by Catherine Gayle

Breakaway	Defensive Zone
On the Fly	Power Play
Taking a Shot	Rain Dance
Light the Lamp	Neutral Zone
Delay of Game	Twice a Rake
Double Major	Saving Grace
In the Zone	Merely a Miss
Holiday Hat Trick	Wallflower
Comeback	Pariah
Dropping Gloves	Seven Minutes in Devon
Bury the Hatchet	Flight of Fancy
Home Ice	Rhyme and Reason
Smoke Signals	Thick as Thieves
Mistletoe Misconduct	An Unintended Journey
Losing an Edge	To Enchant an Icy Earl
Ghost Dance	The Devil to Pay
Dreaming Up a Dare	A Dance with the Devil
Game Breaker	Wanton Wives
Rites of Passage